# Holly's Heart

## by

## Melinda Sanchez

*Christmas Frost, Book 3*

**Holly's Heart**

COPYRIGHT © 2019 by Melinda Sue Sanchez

Cover Art by *Kristian Norris*

The Wild Rose Press, Inc.
PO Box 708
Adams Basin, NY 14410-0708
Visit us at www.thewildrosepress.com

Publishing History
First Sweetheart Rose Edition, 2019
Print ISBN 978-1-5092-2923-9
Digital ISBN 978-1-5092-2924-6

*Christmas Frost, Book 3*
Published in the United States of America

Elam took me by the hand and gently tugged me in his direction; I floated up on the couch beside him.

He rubbed my arm. "Holly, you feel cold." He lay down and pulled me back against his chest, his arms wrapped around me.

Minutes crawled by while I struggled to breathe normally.

"I can feel your heartbeat through your back," he whispered.

"I'm a little—"

His breath had warmed the back of my neck. "Are you warmer now?"

A shiver rippled over my skin from my toes to my head. "Almost," I managed.

"Almost isn't good enough." He leaned up on one elbow, looking down at me and stroking the side of my face with his fingertips. "You are incredibly beautiful, Holly. No wonder Marco went after you."

I rolled over on my back and looked up into his eyes. "There is no…"

He leaned down and skimmed his lips over mine in a friendly kiss. "I am so happy you came this weekend."

I tilted my chin and gently kissed him back. Elam, Elam, Elam…"So am I." I wanted more. I yearned for more. I shivered again.

Elam cleared his throat, moved over and stood up. "It is cold in here." He grabbed my pillow and the blanket off the floor and spread it over me. "I'm not sure L.A. warmed you up as much as you'd hoped."

"Maybe nothing is as much as I'd hoped."

**The Christmas Frost Series**

*FINDING JOY*
*NOELLE'S KISS*
*HOLLY'S HEART*
*CHRISSY'S CATCH*

These are the stories of the four Frost sisters, who overcome heartache, betrayal and ghosts from the past to find true love and bring back the magic of Christmas.

## Dedication

To my mother,
Who kept me going through
the years of unrequited love.
And to my husband,
Who made it all worth it.

Chapter One

Tiny sparkles in the tile reflected light in the dim hallway as I passed between rooms. Numerous vital checks, and a dozen doses of medicine later, I welcomed a ten-minute break before I tackled the paperwork—mounds and mounds of paperwork.

The door to the employee lounge expelled a soft gush of air as I entered, looking to quiet my hunger pangs with a stale treat from the vending machine. I peered closely to choose between an apple and a strawberry granola bar, and someone came up from behind and poked me in the ribs. I let out a squeal and spun around to the laughing face of my coworker, Alice. We cupped our hands over our mouths. If we woke the patients at 3:00 in the morning, we would spend the next several hours getting them all settled again.

"What are you thinking? You'll get us both fired," I whispered.

Alice stood half a head shorter than me and her curls bobbed as she stifled her giggle. "You almost jumped a mile."

"You almost gave me a heart attack."

"Well, you are in the right place for it, anyway. But what are you doing working another night shift, Holly? You work more overtime and late shifts than any nurse I know. You have seniority, you know."

"There's such a high demand in pediatrics. They needed someone."

"Ehh—like I said, you are covering for this shift too much. Maybe you need someone, Holly. Someone at home you don't want to leave at night."

I smiled. "My cat? Oh, she's fine. But seriously, sometimes I want to be here late like this."

"Yeah, right." She smirked.

"I do, especially here in pediatrics. The empty quiet is too spooky for some of these kids. Their little whispery voices and soft, pudgy hands get to me. I like giving comfort in the middle of their lonely nights."

Alice and I both looked over in surprise when someone sat up on the couch in the back of the lounge.

"You need a man, honey. Good—bad—it don't matter, as long as it's a man."

I looked into the plump face and dark eyes of our nurse's aide, Mrs. Torres, and put my hands on my hips. "I've got people sneaking up on me all over in this place. I didn't know it would be so scary in here."

She shook her head. "No, honey, you need to hear what I say. You want to give comfort so much? That means you need comfort. You need a man."

I cleared my throat and pushed the hair that had come loose from my ponytail back behind my ear. "Ha. Well, you may be right. But nowadays I wonder if I'd be better off to forget men altogether."

Her eyes narrowed and she pursed her lips. "Oh dear, you got it worse than I feared. You are in love with a man who breaks your heart." She wiggled to her feet. "I've been an aide here a long, long time, and I seen you come and go, come and go, all the time. You are too lonely, Miss Holly."

My words froze for a moment before I opened my mouth to protest again, sure that I'd given her the wrong impression. But she walked up, shaking her head and waved her hand in front of my face to shush me.

"You stare in space with those big eyes like that; I know what I see." She scribbled something on the back of a patient's menu card someone had left on the coffee table and handed it back to me. "Here is my number. My Pablo is not married. He is going bald and is a little lazy, but he has a good heart."

The break room door closed behind Mrs. Torres when she left, and Alice and I had our hands over our mouths again, stifling a laugh.

"I didn't know I was so transparent," I whispered.

Alice's eyes widened before she headed out of the lounge. "You better watch out; Pablo may show up during your shift with a bouquet of roses one of these days."

I laughed and shook my head before I turned back to the vending machine. Mrs. Torres loved to mother the young nurses, but at age twenty-eight I'd certainly learned a few things about my own life and knew my own feelings. There was no way I was "transparent" because of a broken heart. Those days were long gone, sewn up and tossed, wrapped and buried, resolved and finished. *Fini*, as I'd learned to say in France last year.

I chose the apple granola bar and washed it down with bottled water. It hit my stomach in a lump.

A large picture window framed the end of the hall, and I stopped to look outside when I left the lounge. Occasional codes chimed over the speaker system throughout the hospital, followed by pages for various doctors and calls for emergencies. No wonder the children woke up so often in the night.

Three more minutes left on my break. I gazed out the huge window. A thin layer of snow settled on the lawn in front of the hospital, and I rubbed my arms to ward off the chill it inspired. February in Colorado Springs can be pretty cold.

I loved this hospital. And my job, despite the questions people asked me all the time about how I could stand the gory parts of being a nurse.

Alice came back up and nudged me. "You've gotten quiet all of a sudden."

"Then I'm surprised you didn't try to make me jump again."

"I can't risk my job any more tonight. And, I've got a problem with one of the patients." Her dimpled cheeks lowered in a frown. "It's that little six-year-old, Jamie Cook. She isn't getting better, and in spite of my usual rule about getting too attached, I'm worried about her."

I rubbed my arms again. "That's why I only work as a substitute in the pediatric ward. I don't have the strength to keep myself professionally focused if I work with the children too long."

"You're the most focused and efficient nurse at this hospital."

"Glad I've got you fooled." I looked up and down the halls of the pediatric floor. "You know why I really love pediatrics, even though I can't stand to work here full time."

She looked out the window beside me. "Yes. I know you lost your baby brother. I'm so sorry. But I would bet that when your family's new children's wing is built and dedicated, you're going to want to work in it full time."

"I just might." I watched a street sweeper roll by, the yellow light on top blinking and its headlights illuminating the huge, empty field where the pediatrics wing would go. "I may never want to leave, if it makes me feel closer to my parents and brother."

"It will." She patted my shoulder. "They will be guardian angels over everyone who comes through those doors." She put her arm around me and hugged me.

I wiped at my eyes and hugged her back. "I can't wait."

I was thirteen and our baby brother Nicholas only nineteen months old when his little heart couldn't take any more strain or attempts to repair its defects, and he slipped away with the angels. He'd been on the way to a cardiac specialist in Denver, but it was too late.

The project for a new pediatric wing at the hospital had been our parents' endeavor. A state-of-the-art center to help and save all the children they could in honor of and dedicated to Nicholas. A car accident had taken our parents before the plans were finished or all the funds were raised to start building. My sisters and I had taken up the cause and would see that wing completed in the name of our parents and little Nicholas. I longed for the day.

\*\*\*\*

My shift ended and I headed to my locker and changed into my running clothes.

The soft glow of daybreak filled the sky with one huge breath of fresh air. Going for a run this early on an icy morning made my muscles tingle as oxygen rushed through my veins like a river released from a dam.

Warmth flooded my skin.

Until four years ago, I had run every morning with my father from the time I was nine years old. I thought of him—and missed him—every time I headed out.

My night shift in the pediatric ward ended at six a.m., and a long run had been the perfect antidote for my tired limbs. I rounded the last corner for home and glanced at my watch. Seven o'clock. I had time to call my sister, Joy, and ask how the plans were coming for the hospital wing before she took her boys to school.

"Come on over," she said when she answered my call. "I couldn't sleep, so I got up at five and started some slices of bread soaking for French toast. I bet you're hungry."

My stomach rumbled. No one cooked French toast like Joy. "I'll take a five-minute shower and be right there."

"You better hurry. I know three little boys who will gobble it all up if you don't get here quick enough."

"Yikes—hide some in the microwave for me." I threw the phone on my bed, grabbed a set of clean clothes and hustled to the shower.

Joy's house, which had been our parents' house and family home, always smelled like fresh-baked bread, whether she just baked or not. The air around her wafted of warm buttered rolls or cinnamon bread.

Three rowdy boys tackled me the minute I walked through Joy's front door. I sat flat on the floor and wrapped my arms around five-year-old Charlie and the three-year-old twins, Mitchell and Micah. "Man oh man, I think you've all grown a foot in a week."

Charlie gave out a war cry and pushed me back till I lay on the floor, and then the twins jumped in to hold me down. "Help! Help!" I cried in a high-pitched voice. "I've been captured by aliens!"

Charlie leaned over my face and held my cheeks with his hands. "And we will never let you go."

"Oh yes you will," yelled Joy from the kitchen. "It's time to clean up and get out the door. All of you monkeys get to the bathroom, brush your teeth and wash your hands."

Charlie held up his hands and called back to the kitchen. "We're aliens, Mom. Not monkeys."

I realized why she'd told them to wash their hands after they all ran off to obey their mother's orders. A sticky residue I attributed to maple syrup coated my cheeks where Charlie had held them.

I wet a paper towel and wiped my face clean when I went in the kitchen. Joy was cleaning up, her blonde hair pulled up in a ponytail that swung back and forth while she quickly put peanut butter and jelly away. My dark, wavy hair compared to Joy's streaked, blonde hair was like night and day.

She slipped sandwiches into lunch bags, then gave me a hug, "Your French toast is in the microwave, and the syrup is there in that little pitcher. Eat up," she ordered.

After she grabbed the lunch bags, she stopped and spun around in the doorway. "And hey, I bumped into your friend Cara yesterday, and she asked how you were. And then she said she needed to call you because she wanted to set you up with some great guy at her office."

Her hazel eyes squinted mischievously. "But I told her you weren't over an old relationship."

"Very funny, Joy."

"Actually, it's not so funny. You look a little pale. I'm sorry I teased you."

She paused again, hesitant to continue, and my stomach did a little flip before I answered her. "I'm fine. I'm long over that…or him."

The boys whooped and hollered in the bathroom, over the sound of splashing water.

Joy looked down the hall toward them and then back at me. "I'm sure you're fine. But I didn't even say the man's name and you still turned pale." She gave me a big hug before she hurried down the hall and called back over her shoulder. "I'm sorry, Holly."

She'd taken a few steps before I yelled down the hallway. "It's fine. I'm okay, I'm completely over…that."

"That's what you said. Sounds good to me." Her voice trailed off and one of the boys closed the door behind her with a loud slam.

I took the golden-brown slices of French toast from the microwave, sat down at the table and stared out the window. The cinnamon goodness failed to diminish the pain in my heart. Thank goodness Mrs. Torres couldn't see my eyes.

\*\*\*\*

Mona Lisa meowed the minute I unlocked my apartment door, but I didn't pet her or fill her bowl. I headed straight for my overstuffed chair, flopped down and pressed my fingers over my eyes.

The cat jumped up on my lap and stretched her front legs across my stomach until her claws extended and poked through my shirt. I pulled her into my arms and buried my face in her soft fur. "At least you love me. Right, Mona?"

I became a cat lady last year. Or at least that's what my "best friend" Elam Holmes had named me when he came for my birthday. I'd turned twenty-eight, still single and I bought myself a kitten for my birthday. He laughed and hugged me around the neck, "Holly, you've entered the twilight zone of cat ladies."

I chortled in response and resisted the urge to scream and kick him in the shins. He had, after all, come all the way to Colorado for my birthday. "You and your 'zones'. I haven't entered any zone. "I just love"—I took a quick glimpse into the bottomless depth of his eyes—"animals."

Mona purred and buried her face in my neck. I'd gone to Europe last summer with my friends, Shelly and Cara, so I named the little ball of black fur Mona Lisa after the...well, everyone knew who she was named after. I flew home from Paris convinced that I was born in the wrong country in the wrong century, and in love with Leonardo Da Vinci. It became a nice diversion. A small reprieve from my empty love life.

I got up and poured fresh food and water in Mona Lisa's dishes, and she rubbed up against my legs before she dove in.

Maybe it had never been real love with Elam. Maybe it had been this twisted, sick obsession that had made me go crazy, and everyone knew I was insane but me. A couple of tears pushed their way out of the dam my fingers had tried to make. I'd totally moved on from Elam. Maybe I did need to call Mrs. Torre's son, Pablo.

## Chapter Two

I met Elam Holmes in the third grade. We became best friends, and only friends. And by the time we turned eighteen, I'd asked the angels a hundred times why, if friendship was our only destiny, they made his mouth so perfect. His lips full. His jaw so strong that the sight of him munching an apple made me stutter and stumble.

Because that had led to my undoing—picking and eating apples in an orchard with Elam Holmes the summer after our high school graduation.

We picked several bushels of apples before rain poured down and soaked us both within minutes. The rows between the trees rushed like miniature rivers, and we slipped and slid our way under the canopy of the apple stand that Elam's family owned. My teeth chattered and my arms hurt from carrying the full basket I still carried in my arms.

Elam put a crate on a table and took the basket from my hands. Instead of setting it down right away, he stood in front of me and smiled. "Wow, Holly. You look amazing in the rain." He lifted my braid with one hand and played with the curls at the end. "This storm makes your eyes and hair look almost black." His smile turned into a chuckle. "You look like an enchantress."

I chuckled, too, sure he was teasing—even though his words and the way he played with my braid had jump-started my heart. "I'm soaking wet and a mess. I probably look like someone drove by and splashed a puddle of mud on me."

His eyes grew a little more serious, but he still smiled. "Not at all. You look really beautiful." He took a step closer. "If we hadn't been locked in the friend-zone since forever, I might have to kiss you right now."

My heart had dropped to my feet. Wind whipped at the canvas overhead and whistled through the deluge of rain still pouring from the clouds. I'd almost convinced myself I was hearing things in the storm, that I imagined what Elam had said, but he set the basket of apples on the table, turned around, and our eyes locked on each other.

He stopped smiling and swallowed. Rain still dripped from the ends of his dark hair onto the plaid collar of his shirt. He stared at me so long my knees began to give way. He reached for me and pulled me up against him. "I might have to kiss you anyway."

Our wet clothes warmed together as we held each other for what seemed like an eternity, his whiskers prickling against my cheek. My breathing stopped and everything blurred when Elam closed his lips over mine. I'd still been breathing all right—breathing hard and fast as shock turned into joy. The whir of the rain disappeared as we slipped into more kisses and the honeyed taste of apples filled my senses.

I staggered when Elam stopped, stepped back and shook his head, his eyes dark and opening wide. "Whoa. I didn't mean to... I mean, I'm sorry if I just ruined everything." He touched my cheek with his hand and then let it drop. "I blew it, Holly. I did mean what I said—you are beautiful—but...I gotta go find Sarah.

You have your car here, right? Right. So, it'll be okay. You, or we, better pretend that didn't happen. I'm so sorry—I know I crossed the line." His voice shook as he grabbed his keys from his pocket, jingling them in his hand like an alarm.

"Elam. It's okay. I mean, we both were here and the rain fell and we had to run so then we stood here and our feet were muddy and the wind..." I had no idea what words were coming out of my mouth because I could not quit staring at his lips. Wow—I had no idea they were that powerful. I could hardly stand without swaying.

His thick brows lowered and he grasped my arm to hold me steady. "You know that friendship zone you created a couple of years ago?"

My cheeks still burned. "Yes..." My voice came out shaky.

"Well, I think it was for the best, Holly. I mean, look at this apple stand. It's the only income my family has. It's a great business and life, but not a big money maker. We come from different worlds." He looked at me in earnest and his speech slowed. "So, you made the right call."

I shook my head to argue with him, completely confused. I didn't care for a second if he had a dime or a million dollars in the bank, and I had no idea what it had to do with us. But he took another step backward. "Sarah is like me, Holly. And she's probably waiting for me by now. I gotta go pick her up."

He ran out from under the canopy but turned around one more time before he got to his beat-up truck. "I'm sorry I messed up. We're still best friends, right?"

I nodded and forced a weak smile.

As soon as he'd driven away, I sank down in the mud.

That happened more than ten years ago and I'm still stuck in that mud. All through the years my head and heart have stayed on a roller coaster, jammed in the on position.

It was my fault. I'm the one who put up the walls and established the whole friend zone all the way back in high school. Even two years before high school graduation. We were sixteen, practically kids, when Elam had tried to ask me out. I was sure back then that the earth orbited around a popular guy named Sam Owens, who had taken me to prom. Sam seemed great, but by the time I realized the mistake I'd made, Elam had moved on to Sarah. After that, I never found a window to even hint I wanted more.

And boy, did I want more. When it was too late. When Elam had walked into the friend zone, he locked the door behind him. And once he did, a fog cleared and I realized how empty I had become. Behind that door was a home I'd always taken for granted, the shelter where I could be anyone I wanted to be, and Elam would still love and accept me.

When I first met Elam, he ignored me. But one day he darted around the corner, where I hid from the playground attendant to climb the big mulberry tree. I scowled at the invader for discovering my secret. "Go back or the teacher will see you. And don't tell on me."

His eyes squinted in the sun. "I'm not gonna tell. Ever."

He climbed up in the tree beside me and we'd been best friends ever since. Until I shunned him for the popular guy in high school and something inside him had withdrawn. We'd spent countless hours together and laughed like we always had. But he had a reserve I couldn't tear down with a bulldozer.

On the day we'd kissed in the apple orchard, I knew he felt it, too—the wall falling down, the way the thunder rumbled inside us. And every time we'd been together since and played our "friends only" roles, a power burned between us right under the surface. But if I took a step in his direction, he took two back. So I stood on the sidelines and watched him make Sarah, and the whole line of girls who followed, the luckiest girls in the world.

We almost crossed the boundary a few years ago. But if I let myself think of that time, a black cloud suffocated me all over again—the days following the fatal car accident that took both my father and mother from me and my three sisters—the day after Christmas. December had always been a charmed month before then, extra magical for all four of us Frost sisters because we had birthdays in that month. We'd always carried our Christmas names with pride—Joy, Noelle, Holly and Chrissy. Until that one December 26th took the two people we all loved most in the world.

Elam had raced back to town the minute he heard about the accident. He held me and let me sob on his shoulder and sleep on his lap for three days in a row. My three sisters and I each cocooned ourselves in our pain in a different way, and I'm not sure I would've survived those first few days without Elam. But he had to go back to college before I could see through the dark glass that stood between me and the rest of the world. However, since that time, even in the midst of terrible darkness, I knew I truly loved Elam Holmes.

I'd returned to nursing school and lost myself in the daily demands of life while Elam had earned his bachelor's degree and then worked hundreds of miles and millions of people away.

He finally came back to the Springs for my birthday. We'd been in touch through texts and emails, but it had been an eternity since I'd seen him. It took one second before the flood of feelings threatened to knock me over. Elam grabbed me up and swung me around while we both laughed. He looked down and kissed me right on the mouth. His eyes widened and he stepped back with a chuckle. "You are even more beautiful, Holly. As if that's possible." He played with the curls of my hair that hung over my shoulder.

He had graduate-class finals waiting back in L.A., and only a day and a half in town to visit his whole family. There was no time to explore anything but friendship. At my birthday dinner he'd stayed at my side and rubbed my arm several times.

Before he headed out the door, he gave me a watch for my gift. "I know how you hate winter, so if things get too cold and too difficult here, then set a date and come see me in L.A. to warm up."

He pulled me against him and held me so long I was sure I'd melted into him. Or at least my tears had wet the front of his jacket. I tried to hold on, but he finally had to go. He handed me his handkerchief and kissed me on each cheek. His eyes were filled with tears, too, and he cupped my face in his hand. Warmth seared between us again. I knew it. It rumbled like the thunder in the apple orchard years before.

Elam stayed at the door, his eyes and mood sober.

He still held my face in his hand and I held my breath as he spoke. "You are an amazing woman, Holly. Let me know if some lucky guy snatches you up before I see you again."

He walked out the door, and when it closed, my heart tumbled over a cliff.

Chapter Three

I cried myself dry. Then extended my running from three to five miles a day, and began dating again. A lot. It takes a huge quota to fill a heart with a hole in the bottom. But I tried; Leonard the grocery clerk, Tyler the jock who spent every date talking about football, Dallin the doctor who loved the fact that I was a nurse and we could work together someday, and Marco the European with the Italian accent who'd given me loads of practice on kissing skills.

I called it quits with Marco when my sister Elle came bursting into my apartment late one night in her designer sweats and found Marco and me ignoring the movie I'd put on and kissing with *gusto* on the couch. She put her hands on her hips and gave Marco a stare-down that said he better back off of her sister before she kicked him in the *pantaloni*. He'd actually bowed and then kissed his fingertips like every Romeo in the movies, then waved goodbye and hurried out the front door.

Elle immediately shifted her glare in my direction. "What are you thinking, Holly?" She marched around the room in her wool house slippers and flipped her blonde hair as she turned each lamp to its brightest setting. "You told me you didn't even have feelings for this guy or like him. Do you think hiding in the shadows and numbing yourself with empty affection is going to fix anything?" She plopped down in a chair across from where I sat staring at the floor, her arms tightly folded. "Do you want to end up like me? Ripped to shreds by some idiot Romeo? You know you are better than that, so stop it already."

I'd leaned back and rested my head on a couch cushion to stare at the ceiling instead of her laser-beam eyes. "Okay, okay, Elle, I get it. I'm shallow and a fool. Does that make you happy? I admit my life sucks and I can't get it back to normal since Mom and Dad died. And nothing I do seems to fix every other broken piece of me, either."

She finally exhaled long and slow in the way I knew meant she was cooling off and calming down. "What do you mean. 'every other broken piece of you?' Huh, I wish I had half of the good life you have."

I shot the laser beams in her direction. "Maybe you've had to fight your battles so long you don't even bother trying to see what others are going through. Just shows what you know." I regretted my ugly words the minute I saw the wave of pain wash over her face. Her ex-husband's infidelity and abuse had led to a nasty divorce and left her to raise her baby girl on her own. Elle covered her eyes with her hands as all of us sisters did when we were trying to hold in our emotions.

I scooted forward on the couch and put my hand on her knee. "I'm sorry, Elle. I didn't mean that. You've been through so much I can't even bear to think about it, let alone go through it." I bit my lip, hard. "Agh, I am shallow."

"You aren't shallow, Holly. We've all been through a lot. But what did you mean about other broken parts of you?"

It was my turn to exhale long and slow. "Nothing. I'm just upset, I guess."

She stood up and lowered her brow. "I can see there is more to it than that, and I'm guessing it still has to do with Elam Holmes, but I've harassed you enough for tonight." She wrapped her arms around me, and the familiar warmth reassured me in ways that a hundred kisses from Marco never could, although I had to admit he had mastered the art of the *baci* in ways I'd never dreamed of. But those kisses left me cold.

After Noelle left, I walked into the bathroom and spat in the sink. Then I made a vow as I stared at the lady in the mirror. "No more mind numbing make-outs for you, Holly Frances Frost."

Chapter Four

A freak snowstorm struck in April, and I sighed on my way to work. I parked in the hospital employee parking lot and stepped out into freezing wind that burned my bare hands and neck. I searched my bag for my scarf.

The day at work promised to be just another line-up of stubborn veins that dodged needles and cranky patients who complained about all their aches and pains. Sheesh, even my job and the people I usually enjoyed had plunged into a frozen dungeon with me. I had to get a grip.

I needed some sunshine and warmth to thaw my heart before I froze to death inside and out. I paused on the word sunshine and my blood raced before my brain had caught up with it; Elam had invited me to visit him in California any time I wanted a break from the cold. I should be fine—I'd cried out the pain over unrequited love, and Elam and I had handled the "friend zone" for forever. I could handle this. If some hidden part of me still pined like an adolescent over him, I had to let that go.

On my first break, I hurried to the lounge, where we had an employee computer, held my breath and sent Elam a message.

****

The pink glow from the sign outside the window lit

up our table at The Mason Jar the next night. No matter how hard or crazy my life got, I could get my feet back under me in two hours of "Frost Sisters Therapy."

We sat at our usual booth, sipped on diet colas, and a health food shake in Elle's case, and munched on salad.

Joy narrowed her eyes and shook her hair back out of her face. "You're flying out to see him? Why doesn't Elam come here? How many years does it take for this guy to wake up?" She rolled her eyes, which happened often when she spoke of Elam.

I winced and tried to think of a way to change the subject that we'd hashed to death a hundred times.

Elle sat across from me and got that mischievous look in her eye like she was about to show someone's underwear to the whole class. "You would think you were both still at a seventh-grade dance, with boys on one side of the room and girls on the other, and everyone is too scared to cross the floor. Why don't you grab the man and lay one on him? Heaven knows that Italian, Marco, should have given you plenty of practice."

I scowled at her "You know you could keep some parts of my life private, dear sister."

Chrissy looked up from her salad, her eyes wide. "What Marco guy, Elle?"

"I guess I'm not supposed to say. I assumed everybody knew."

"Knew what?" asked Joy.

"Knew that Holly here was tickling tonsils with an Italian playboy named, Marco," said Elle with a wink.

"Tickling tonsils? Playboy? What is this, the 1950s?" I rolled my eyes.

Elle had snickered and sucked down more of her "health conscious" energy drink. "Don't dodge the issue here. The point is that you know what you really want, so go for it."

At that point I crumpled my napkin and threw it at Elle. "I don't think I even feel attracted to Elam anymore. If Elam feels something more, then I want him to go for it. Or at least show he wants to. I've lived with the fear that if I tried to make a move and he only feels friendship for me, I might get my heart broken. Plus lose my best friend forever."

Elle threw the napkin back at me and it bounced off my arm. "You've held back because of fear for far too long. You could be here for the next decade waiting for the perfect scenario in the perfect order. Maybe, since you two have shared every other secret in your lives for twenty years—and you're both adults—you should just talk to the man and let it all hang out."

Joy perked up. "Yes, let it all hang out."

"Oh good. We've made our way to the 1960's. Let's be groovy and let it all hang out." I wanted this conversation to end, right now.

"Are you going to focus on fear and sarcasm, or on how to get Elam to finally realize and admit he's loved you since the third grade?" asked Chrissy, her big hazel eyes softened with compassion.

My shoulders slacked and I covered my face with my hands. Our youngest sister was gentle and soft spoken, but when she decided to speak up, she really nailed an issue on the head.

She patted me on the shoulder. "Elle is right. Come on, Holly—no matter what you've tried, you've always come back to the fact that you have unresolved feelings for Elam. Go see if it will work out, once and for all."

I uncovered my face. "I know he's felt more than just friendship for me all these years, too, but then he flips around and goes the other way. I can't take the risk of any more pain. If Elam wants more, then I'm hoping he'll be the one to do something more while I'm there."

"Hoping?" asked Joy. "If there is one thing I've learned from losing Tom, there is no sense wasting one minute of time that you could be with the one you love. Don't sit back and hope, Holly, make it happen. Look for the right moment, place or circumstance, and change your life. You've been hurting for years."

I closed my eyes. "Okay, okay. I know you're all right. I'll do it. I'll let it all hang out."

Truth was a great motivator. I could do this.

One phone call completed, one airline ticket purchased online and soon we'd have liftoff. Here we go, Holly, I told myself. Do not blow it...

\*\*\*\*

I chewed my nails during the whole flight to L.A. like I'd reverted to third grade again. When the plane landed, I waited until almost all the other passengers had gone before I made my way down the aisle to the exit. Security had blocked anyone from meeting passengers at the gate, so I had a long walk down the hall to work on my nerves.

And then I spotted him. He stood at the doorway to baggage claim, his hands in the back pockets of his jeans, his dark hair curled over the edge of his collar. A slow smile spread on his face when he saw me, like he had all the time in the world to just stand there looking gorgeous. I'd seen that stance a thousand times, and it never failed to slam my heart against my ribcage. We hugged, and within those few seconds of Elam's arms around me and the tickle of his whiskers against my cheek, the balmy air of Los Angeles had begun to warm my bones.

I glanced over at Elam as we walked to his car. "I can see why you love it here. I wish I could bottle some of this warmth and take it home with me." I glanced at him again. "But you're wearing your Levi jacket. Do people actually feel cold in Los Angeles?"

He laughed over the sound of the wheels of my suitcase bumping over the asphalt of the airport parking lot. "I don't, not at all. But I miss the changing seasons, so this old jacket makes me feel more at home." He hooked his arm around my neck and pulled me against him as we walked, and I caught the scent of the sandalwood soap he always used. I inhaled deeply.

"Plus my best friend, Holly bought it for me years ago, remember?"

I caught my breath. "Oh, yes. Of course, I remember. Your twenty-fourth birthday, right? I'm glad you still like it. I should have brought you a bottle of cold air from home or something to go with it."

"You brought yourself and that's good enough for me."

Okay, this was going to be good.

****

His apartment looked small but a lot nicer than I'd expected for a grad student. "You live here by yourself?"

"Nah, I have a roommate named Brandon, but he works odd hours so I hardly see him. And he's on vacation for the next two weeks, so I have the place to myself."

He carried my suitcase into his bedroom and tossed it up on his bed. I caught up and shook my head. "Wait a minute, I told you I would sleep on the couch, remember? I don't want to kick you out of your room."

He gazed over at me with those heavy-lidded eyes and a smirk on his face. "Who said you're kicking me outta my room?"

I stared at the queen-sized bed and heat rose up my neck. I chuckled or choked—not sure which. "Ha ha, very funny, buddy." If only…I grabbed my suitcase and pulled it toward the door. "I am taking the couch."

He got to the door before I did and put his hand over mine where I gripped the suitcase handle. "Holly, I was teasing you." His smirk grew into a wide grin. "I know you are a virtuous woman."

I punched him in the arm. "Stop. You make it sound like a bad thing." And if you only knew how much I…

"Well, I'm sure for all the guys, who I know must be knocking at your door, it is a 'bad' thing."

I punched him again and he laughed and rubbed at his bicep. "Ouch. Dang, woman. Lifting patients and giving shots must give you super strength." His eyes grew more serious and he tapped me a few times on the nose with his pointer finger. "Be nice, Holly-wood."

"Oh, my gosh, you haven't called me that in ages."

"I do in my head." He pointed out the window with a view to the mountains. "See the famous sign up there? Hollywood. Every time I see it I think of you."

I left my suitcase in the bedroom and plopped down on his couch. "Thank goodness for that sign or you may have forgotten me by now." I smiled but the idea of Elam possibly forgetting me gave me a flashback to the loneliness I had battled without him. I grabbed a pillow beside me and played with the fringe around the edges to keep my hands busy.

Elam had sat down in a chair across from the couch and stared at me so long I stopped breathing. He propped his feet on the coffee table. "You know I could never forget you, Holly. You're my tree-climbing buddy, remember?"

I may learn to hate the word "buddy." I smiled. "Oh, I remember. Some things you never forget."

His gaze had drifted to my mouth and stayed there. "Yep, some things you never forget."

The gold in his hazel eyes caught a reflection of light that dazzled me like a school girl. Come on, Holly, face it like a woman.

Elam jumped up. "Would you like something to drink? Some water or a soda or something?"

"Sure. Any of the above."

A collage of pictures covered half of his front room wall; Elam and kids of all ages, grinning and laughing at the zoo, a picnic, a museum, on the bus, and several in the classroom. It went on and on, and the tenderness almost made me dizzy.

I pointed at them. "It's obvious those kids love you." And I don't blame them...

"I love what I do and the kids are the best part. I'm just lucky."

"It's not luck, it's a gift. The kids are the lucky ones." I studied more of the pictures. "I thought you taught junior high? There are kids of all ages here."

"I didn't tell you? I changed my master's degree to hospital administration. But I'm also an assistant director at the Boys and Girls Club here in Los

Angeles. The pictures are from there."

"Wow, that's great. I had no idea you'd changed your MBA emphasis. But hospital admin is a great field. And the Boys and Girls Club—what a wonderful thing to do."

He shrugged his shoulders. "Well, thanks. But it's nothing elaborate or fancy; just some sports, some fun and programs to get their imaginations going and encourage them all we can."

I looked at the rows of smiling kids again. "Your hard work is paying off."

He scratched at the scruff of dark whiskers on his cheeks. "I love it. Although you're right, it is a lot of work." He smiled and winked at me. "But I couldn't just pick apples for a living, could I?"

My heart had jumped with the memory of kissing Elam at his parents' orchard, and the pain of watching him run off to Sarah. I searched for words. "No…I guess you wanted something different."

His eyes had turned solemn. "What we want and what we can have don't always match up. We have to search other horizons." He pointed at the pictures. "This has been a good horizon. I'm grateful for it."

A different and 'good' horizon, far away from me. He'd chosen this; he wanted this place and other women—every other woman but me. I had a sudden urge to run.

But I stayed on the couch, and he brought me a club soda. "You ever hear from Sam Owens?"

"From high school?" I almost dropped my drink.

He lowered one brow. "I seem to recall that you hooked up with him after high school, and for quite a while."

"You mean, while you were with Sarah at college? Yes, I dated Sam again in college, as you well know. And we never 'hooked up,' either. It wasn't a love match."

"Neither was Sarah."

"Bah! You were pretty down when you broke up, as I remember, and you dated her for three years. You didn't know it wasn't a love match for that long?"

"I'm a slow learner."

"No, you aren't." The words had come out flat and landed on the floor between us, and I couldn't force myself to smile. Years of stabbing pain flooded me like a tidal wave; the endless days and nights I knew he'd spent with Sarah, and the others who'd followed, while I cried in my pillow or lived a hollow happiness with others.

Elam watched me without blinking. "That's a pretty serious expression on your face. Was that a compliment or are you upset with me?"

I shook my glass and rattled the ice in my drink. "What would I have to be upset about?"

"I hope nothing, but for a minute there I wasn't too sure."

The corners of my mouth had still refused to lift. Maybe I was going to lose it and burst into tears in the first hour we spent together. Come on, Holly, you can't blurt out your feelings while drowning in bad memories.

Elam took a few gulps of his drink and set it on a coffee table. "Are we okay? I have this weird feeling, like we've had our first fight or something.

I crossed my legs and leaned back on the couch. "First? Hardly."

"We've fought before?"

"Humpft."

Elam lifted his eyebrows. "If we've fought before, I didn't know about it."

"Maybe there's a lot you didn't know." I knew I sounded odd, maybe even rude, but pent-up frustration climbed up my throat. I swallowed.

"You said I'm not a slow learner, but then there's a lot I don't know. Have I been dense all these years? Why don't you tell me?"

I bit my bottom lip and then looked out the window. "We all have to solve our own mysteries."

"Give me a hint."

The knot in my stomach refused to let up. I wanted to yell at him. To throw things at him for not wanting more from me, never choosing me over the many women he'd dated. I stood up and walked past the pictures of the children and teenagers from the club. I looked closely at their smiling faces and my breathing finally eased. I sipped on my drink and managed to smile, like I'd been teasing him all along.

Elam's shoulders relaxed. "Really, Holly, you seemed furious with me over something."

I kept smiling. "No way—what would I have to be mad about?"

Good grief—maybe I didn't have any guts at all.

Chapter Five

Elam won and insisted I sleep in his room. His feet stuck out over the end of the couch, but he stretched out and yawned. I, on the other hand, could not sleep with him so close after missing him for months.

I tip-toed into the front room when I was sure he'd fallen asleep. The curtains at the window were partway open and let light from a lamp post outside stream in. It gave the room a surreal glow and made Elam's face look like an angel's.

I eased myself into a chair and watched him sleep with a peace I could only dream of. My arms ached to wrap themselves around him and I traced every angle of his face in my mind. I stared at his wide shoulders and imagined what it would be like to lie beside him with my head resting on his chest. The tightness in my stomach turned into knots. I slipped back into the bedroom and pulled the covers over my head.

****

Nothing warmed the bones and lightened the heart like "The Happiest Place on Earth." I'd never been to Disneyland, and Elam grinned like a kid as he shuffled me inside and began the tour the next morning. He bought me a pair of Mickey Mouse ears at the first gift stand we came to inside the gates and placed them on my head. "Here you go. All first timers have to wear these or they won't let you on any of the rides."

We started walking while I put on the ears. "What? How would they know it's my first time coming here?"

"They have experts who know exactly how to read body language. There are hidden cameras throughout the park and this team of people watch and report when they spot a newbie." He pointed to the tops of several buildings where cameras might be.

I stopped and put my hands on my hips. "No way. How could they possibly know that I'm a 'newbie'?"

He smirked and tapped me on the nose again. "Because you're wearing Mickey Mouse ears."

"Oh you!" I tried to punch him in the arm but he ran backwards.

"Wait, Holly, the team of experts will see you. If you punch someone, they won't let you on any of the rides."

I chased him farther until a band that looked like it had stepped out of the 1940s began playing in the middle of a plaza. I looped my arm through Elam's as I always did, and we watched them play.

By the end of the day my feet ached but I hardly noticed. We laughed, screamed, ate ice-cream cones as big as a mountain and rode every ride at least twice. I was exhausted and happier than I'd been in years. I hugged Elam. "Thank you for a most magical day. You are my best friend all over again."

My sisters would slap themselves on the forehead because I'd used the term "best friend." Holly, act and talk like a woman—not a teenager. Their voices rang in my head.

Elam hugged me back and kept his hands on my shoulders as he looked at me. "You are welcome, Holly-wood." His brows lowered and his smile faded.

He tapped me on the nose…again.

"You sure like touching my nose this trip. Do I have something on my face you're trying to tell me about?"

He smiled and put his hands back on my shoulders. "I've always liked your nose."

And I've always loved the feel of your hands on my shoulders. Or when you touch me anywhere, for that matter. "Thank you. I'm not sure I've ever heard you say that before."

He shrugged and dropped his hands. "Oh, I'm full of surprises."

I wondered how surprised he'd be if I leaned in and kissed him like I'd been dying to since I got off the plane.

****

It's sad how predictable I was—my favorite ride of the entire day had been the Matterhorn. Not because of the thrill of the roller-coaster or the "scary" abominable snowman, but because I sat in front of Elam in our sled and leaned back on his chest through the whole thing. In fact, I insisted that we ride it three times. I screamed extra loud each time we whipped around a corner to be sure I sounded scared enough to really lean into him.

And of course, I was deeply spooked in the Haunted Mansion, startled by the waterfall drops in Pirates of the Caribbean and forced to hold on extra tight on Space Mountain. All of them required as much huddling with Elam as possible.

We rode the teacups three times because it was Elam's favorite ride. He loved to see how fast we could get the teacup spinning. I smiled and laughed like I was having a good time, clear up to the moment we finished round three and I had to stop at the nearest garbage can to throw up the Monte Cristo sandwich I'd had for lunch. It was almost worth it—Elam actually held my hair back for me while I puked, and he hugged me after I finished. He kept his arm around me and walked me all the way to the bathroom. I took off at a run when we reached the door before my stomach unleashed round two of the Monte Cristo debacle on the sidewalk.

**** 

"He said he's always liked my nose." I made a call to Chrissy for moral support while I recovered for a moment in the bathroom.

"That's it? After a whole night, last night, and spending all day together, he holds your hair back while you throw up and he likes your nose?" sighed Chrissy.

"Agh. I'm taking what I can get again, aren't I?"

"Yes, you are. I mean, it all sounds sweet-n-cozy, but you aren't seventeen, Holly. You don't have to torture yourself in a spinning teacup to get a man to hug you. You love him. Act like it."

"Okay, okay, I'll express more."

"A lot more."

"You haven't seen him with dozens of other girls right in your face for ten years."

"A lot more, Holly. No excuses."

"I don't think he has those kinds of feelings for me. I'll make a fool of myself."

"Trust me, it won't kill you to be a fool. No excuses."

"I could lose our friendship. It might never be the same again."

"Or you might have everything you've ever dreamed of. No excuses."

Maybe Chrissy was right—I had a whole foundation with Elam to make me feel reassured. He had taught me how to play guitar and I taught him how to dance. He talked me through many test anxiety episodes while we were in high school. We'd laughed till we snorted at dozens of corny movies and hiked to the top of more than one mountain together. He came on almost every family vacation we'd gone on when we were teenagers. Tomorrow. I would show my feelings tomorrow. I tossed and turned all night. But I slept better than I had the night before.

\*\*\*\*

The next morning, we headed to the beach. I had never swam in the ocean before, so the anticipation gave me a real surge of excitement. I'd been an expert roller-blader in high school, so when I spotted a rental booth for them, I insisted we get some blades and try them out before we headed to the water,

We skated up and down on the long sidewalks that ran beside the rolling waves of the ocean. Elam skated faster than I did and reached back to grab my hand if he got too far ahead.

"I wish we could skate all day," I called out to him as we rounded another curve in the wide sidewalk. A heavenly breeze added to the rush of wind that whistled past. He led me to a lemonade stand and we sat down with icy drinks to catch our breath.

"You run any marathons recently?" he asked.

I gulped down more lemonade. "Nope. It isn't the same without my running partner with me." I winked at him.

"How many of those heel-pounding things did you drag me into, anyway?" He laughed.

"Huh, you loved it and you know it."

He pushed his hair back off his forehead. Man, the guy had perfect bone structure. Thick brows, piercing hazel eyes and that wicked jawline. No matter how many times I'd gazed at it, that jaw and those full lips melted every muscle in my body. Elam chugged down some lemonade and then licked his lips, and I choked on a piece of lemon pulp in my drink. I coughed for air and he jumped up and patted my back until I quit coughing, then ended with a shoulder rub that had me sinking into my chair.

We spread a blanket over the sand to lie down on the beach. Spring was not prime time for swimming, unless you loved frigid water, but I had to give it a try while I had the chance. I wore my bathing suit under my clothes, so I pulled off my jeans and blouse and shivered as my skin adjusted to the damp breeze—as well as the fact that Elam could see me half naked.

I'd been tempted to wear a bikini to really get his attention, but my skin hadn't seen the sun in months and my snowy glow would scare the fish away. I'd settled for my favorite red one-piece with the crisscross straps and left my hair down free to take full advantage of the briny breeze.

"I never realized salt had an aroma before today, but it actually smells like salt out here." I said.

Elam chuckled and tapped my nose. "Cute and observant little nose you have there, Ms. Frost. Although I think the damp and fishy smells rule over any 'salt' aroma."

He brushed his fingers through the strands of my hair. "I like how you've let your hair grow so long. It goes way past your shoulders now."

The feel of his hands in my hair, his sideways glance at me in my suit with his eyebrows raised in appreciation—I feared I'd have to dive into the water to cool off any minute. "Well, thank you. My skin is so pale I definitely don't look like a native Californian."

"Your skin looks smooth as satin. The Californians will be jealous."

"And yours is always naturally tan. No fair."

Elam chuckled and shook his head. He whipped off his shirt and flexed his muscles, posing like a weightlifter in a contest. I laughed, and had to force myself not to gape at his smooth muscles and the sprinkle of hair across his chest. I took a deep breath to ease the tug in my belly.

Elam lay down on the blanket and I lay down beside him and looked up at the thin veil of clouds that floated over us. "I think I could become addicted to the feel of that breeze and the cry of seagulls. Let's live here forever."

He laughed "Didn't you say that when we went with your family to Yellowstone? And I think you said it again at the Grand Canyon." He put his hands behind his head as a pillow. "And besides, I sort of do live here, you know."

I almost panicked. "Sure, but you are planning on coming back to Colorado Springs after you get your Master's, right?"

"Hmmm...I'm not sure what I should do yet. I have some, you know, personal things to figure out first."

"Sounds serious."

"It was. Until three weeks ago."

Nooooo... "What's her name?" I choked.

"Erin."

"Isn't that a boy's name?"

"Be nice."

"Okay, another name that starts with E. What a coincidence."

He laughed. "Yeah, Erin would joke about it and call us 'the two E's' when we'd go places."

The gentle rhythm of the waves whisking over the sand didn't ease the tightness in my throat. I wished the water could wash the name Erin out to sea. "What happened?"

"Oh, you know. Complications."

"Very vague."

"Well, what about you? How's Marco?"

I gasped. "How do you know about, Marco?"

"Geez, don't panic. I have Facebook, remember? If you want to have privacy, don't post selfies with your boyfriends."

"He wasn't my boyfriend."

"Ummm, I do believe you had your lips locked on his in more than one photo."

I sat up and started digging a hole in the sand with my fingers next to the blanket. Maybe, if I dug it deep enough, I could climb in it.

"He was Italian." I stood up and brushed off my hands. "Let's go look for seashells."

"You mean, let's change the subject."

"I'm not trying to hide anything."

"I know; I saw your kissing pictures. But you may want to brush the sand off your backside."

Dang-it. He could still make me blush. I'd toilet-papered houses and lip-synced Britney Spears songs with this guy in junior high. We'd gone through those wonderful "developmental years" together, but I still blushed whenever he commented on my anatomy. I grabbed a towel and wrapped it around my waist as Elam slung the small backpack we'd brought with us over his shoulder.

We headed down to the edge of the water, letting it wash over our feet as we walked. The waves hissed their way up the beach, leaving frothy bubbles behind that soaked into the sand. I gathered sea shells and handed them to Elam to put into the pack. I studied a broken shell, wondering what had made it break or crack as it had flowed through water. It must have tumbled through the waves a million times before it came to rest right at our feet. I rubbed the smooth surface between my finger and my thumb.

I'm keeping this one.

Elam strolled casually, opened a plastic bag in the backpack and pulled out an apple. The flexing muscles in his jaw as he chewed stole my attention from the ocean. Fruit had become the bane of my sanity. If I stopped walking and leaned toward Elam, just a little bit, I might catch a whiff of that apple on his breath…

I closed my eyes for two seconds as we walked, and something sharp jabbed the bottom of my foot. "Ouch!" I grabbed my painful foot and hopped on the other.

Elam stopped. "Sit down so I can look at it." I plunked myself down onto the warm sand and fought back a few totally unnecessary tears that had begun to sting my eyes.

"Whoa, I don't see any bleeding, but this could be bad" he said.

"Seriously?" I gasped, not happy at all that some sea creature might've stung or bit me.

"Well, there are many poisonous and ravenous little critters in the ocean, you know."

Teasing was one of Elam's favorite past times, but he lowered his brow as if sincerely concerned. I stared him down. "Elam, you'd better not be mocking me."

He winked at me and knelt on the sand, taking my foot in his hands. When he ran his long fingers over the arch of my foot and brushed the sand away, my stomach did a little flip.

The examination continued and Elam scowled. "Hmmm, yeah, this doesn't look good at all. I think there was a shark tooth, an old pirates knife or a walrus tusk buried in the sand right here."

I recognized his snarky expression. "A walrus tusk, huh? Wow, that is dangerous." I narrowed my eyes at him and wished we were standing, so I could give him a kick in the shins. I shook off his hands, even though I was sorry to lose his touch, and stood up, keeping my sore foot off the ground.

He chuckled as he stood up beside me.

A wave surged up the sand and rose above my knees. I tried to keep my balance, but it was no use on one leg in shifting sand—I toppled backwards, landing in the rushing water. It whooshed over the top of me before it receded, leaving goose bumps all over my wet skin and my hair dripping down over my face.

Elam stood beside me like the wave hadn't affected his balance at all. He chortled. "I wish you could've seen the surprise on your face when that wave hit." He pulled me up with one hand as I coughed and sputtered.

I tried to get my drenched and tangled hair out of my face, but the more I tried, the more tangled it became. I gave up fighting it.

Another big wave rose up, and this time I forgot my sore foot and flipped my hair back. I ran right for the wave and dove in. The push and pull of the current rolled me in a somersault underwater more than once before it let me come up for air. I swallowed a mouthful of nasty salt water that burned my throat and seared its way straight up my nose. I coughed for air and pushed my way back toward shore, my teeth chattering together and my eyes stinging.

Elam waded out to meet me. "Are you crazy, Holly-wood? The deeper water is wild and there are riptides. And it's freezing cold." He pulled a strand of seaweed from my hair and burst out laughing.

That was enough. I answered him with a hearty shove and he fell straight back onto his backside in the water.

Before he could get up, the next wave had smacked and pitched me forward across Elam's waist, and my face dipped in the water. I came up for air and laughed so hard I couldn't get up. Our arms, elbows and legs jabbed and poked at each other as we struggled for our footing in the rushing water, but a big wave crashed in and ran over the top of us, leaving us rolling toward the shore with our arms gripped around each other.

We came to a stop with Elam over the top of me like a scene from a movie. Our noses bumped and his lips hovered just above mine. The ocean still washed back and forth over our legs, but Elam kept his arms wrapped around me. His hazel eyes looked green as the sea and the water dripped from his hair onto my cheeks. I could barely breathe. I shivered, but not from the cold. This is it, this is it…

Another wave sprayed over us and Elam got to his

feet. He held my hand and led me farther up the beach so we wouldn't be toppled by another wave. We made it back to our blanket and lay down to catch our breath. My towel was long gone in the waves, but our small backpack, with our phones and the car keys in it, had filled with water. Elam emptied the water out of the pack, and I shrugged, sure the phones were toast.

But I didn't care about my ruined phone or even the car keys. I lay on the blanket and looked up at the sky, still flushed over the moment Elam had leaned over me and our faces had been so close. His breath had touched my lips, and his skin brushed against mine.

After a few minutes, Elam sat up. "It's too bad there weren't more people out today to witness your acrobatics."

"Only my acrobatics? I do recall being jabbed more than once by your elbows and knees while you flew around in the waves. People would've had quite the show."

"Yeah, yeah, I admit to a few elbow jabs in the struggle…but," he winked at me and raised his eyebrows suggestively, "some of the struggle was worth it."

I gasped in shock that he actually mentioned our "entanglement," and I couldn't suppress the smile that slowly spread on my face. Elam chuckled at my reaction and I stared at him, not sure if the hint he'd dropped was real. He kept his gaze locked on me; his eyes glinting gold in the sun. His tan skin and dark hair still damp and unruly in the breeze.

I swallowed, "Elam, I think…"

His phone rang. An ocean-soaked, wave-tossed, evil phone rang.

"How?" I managed.

"I put the phones in plastic bags before we got out here. Didn't you see me?"

"No."

He took it out of the bag and sighed when he looked at the screen. "Sorry, Holly. I better get this."

It was her. Erin. Only a woman could make his eyes glaze over the way they had when he saw who was calling. I cursed plastic bags.

Elam stood up and walked down the beach while he talked. At least I didn't have to hear what he said.

I sat up and the breeze stung my eyes. I finally checked my foot. It didn't bleed or hurt anymore, but the rest of me ached every time I glanced at Elam still talking on his phone.

Our suits had almost dried before we made our way back to the car. I put my arm through Elam's, grateful for the chance to hold onto him for one minute. He'd stayed quiet after his phone conversation.

"You okay? You seem sad."

He shrugged and lifted a hand full of my damp sandy hair. "You could pass for a mermaid out here."

My face flushed. "I don't think I looked like a mermaid a little while ago in those waves."

"You're always beautiful, Holly."

My throat tightened. "Thank you, Elam…you were an amazing lifeguard saving me from the waves. My hero."

He shrugged. "That's not what Erin calls me."

And now I was seasick. "So, what happened? You don't have to tell me, but I want to know if you're okay." Because I'm a masochist—agh.

There was no escape, I was going to feel my heart

ebb with the tide as Elam talked about a woman he obviously had feelings for.

"I'm okay." He shrugged.

But the breeze off the ocean had turned cold.

Chapter Six

One more night before my chances ended. I had
moved from point zero to point one on the scale of hope
for anything more than Elam's friendship. I considered
making another sister hotline phone call—but Joy
would be busy getting her kids to bed; Elle would love
a chance to cajole me into action, but my nerves
teetered on the edge and I might explode if pushed. A
fleeting wish always haunted me: if only I could call
my mother. Just the sound of her voice would soothe
me. She'd always known what to do and could coax me
into believing all would be well.

The clock kept spinning and nerves cinched around
my ribs like a corset. I promised myself while we ate
dinner on the pier that I would say or do something to
show Elam I cared...more deeply.

An outdoor juke box played a catchy tune from the
early sixties and people laughed and clanked their beers
together in a toast several tables away. Elam sat across
from me, his gaze shifting back and forth from me to
the waves that crashed against the legs of the pier.

"Did I tell you that Erin is a fellow volunteer at the
Boys' and Girls' Club?" he asked.

The words plunged like a rock to the bottom of my
stomach. That would mean he saw her. A lot.

"No you didn't" I chirped, "She must be nice." I
escaped behind a big bite of my hamburger that

tumbled with the rock in my belly.

Elam closed up on the subject. And I wasn't going to beg for painful conversation. I had to keep a window open to talk about us. But we both stayed quiet all the way back to his apartment, steeling glances back and forth at one another.

****

Elam put on a movie that night. An action movie. I stretched out on one end of the couch, Elam on the other. Seventh grade was back again. At least our feet bumped once in a while in the middle. He dozed off as the movie ended, and I slipped into the bedroom, grabbed a blanket and pillow and lay down on the floor next to the couch where he slept. I had to at least be near him for the few hours we had left before morning.

I dozed on the floor and then woke with a start when Elam slid his hand around my waist and tugged on me. "Come up here—I'm not letting you sleep on the floor," he whispered.

I had to be dreaming, but I was wide awake. Elam pulled on me some more, and the warmth of his hand made my arms and legs tingle. I floated up on the couch.

He sat beside me and touched my arm. "Holly, you feel cold." He lay down and pulled me back against his chest, his arms wrapped around me.

Minutes crawled by while I struggled to breathe normally.

"I can feel your heartbeat through your back," he whispered.

"I'm a little—"

His breath had warmed the back of my neck. "Are you warmer now?"

A shiver rippled over my skin from my toes to my head. "Almost," I managed.

"Almost isn't good enough." He leaned up on one elbow, looking down at me and stroking the side of my face with his fingertips. "You are incredibly beautiful, Holly. No wonder Marco went after you."

I rolled over on my back and looked up into his eyes. "There is no…"

He leaned down and skimmed his lips over mine in a friendly kiss. "I am so happy you came this weekend."

I tilted my chin and gently kissed him back. Elam, Elam, Elam…"So am I." I wanted more. I yearned for more. I shivered again.

Elam cleared his throat, moved over and stood up. "It is cold in here." He grabbed my pillow and the blanket off the floor and spread it over me. "I'm not sure L.A. warmed you up as much as you'd hoped."

"Maybe nothing is as much as I'd hoped."

"What do you mean?"

Someone knocked at the apartment door. It was two o'clock in the morning. It could only be one person.

Elam opened the door and the glare from the front porch light hurt my eyes and illuminated a tall, athletic looking blonde. Erin. An attractive fellow volunteer who would see him every day after I left. Elam stepped out on the porch and shut the door behind him.

And I died on my pillow.

Two hours passed before he came back inside. Each minute that ticked on the clock carried my hopes for Elam and me farther and farther away.

\*\*\*\*

The airport buzzed with people and my flight home

had been called. At least the other "E" hadn't come along to see me off. Elam was definitely more quiet and distant than he'd been all weekend.

I'd decided the night before, when Elam stayed out on the porch with Erin, that this would be my first and last trip to LA. The last time I'd have to fall apart on the inside while acting like everything was fine. The deep longing I had for Elam may never go away. No matter how painful it would be to let our friendship go, I had to do it; I could not do this anymore. I'd have to explain it to him someday, but not now.

\*\*\*\*

I stood next to Elam, looking at the face that had been a part of my heart and soul for most of my life. My pulse pounded clear to my fingertips and a sob inched its way up my throat. This would be goodbye and he wouldn't even know it.

Elam had his arm around my shoulders and patted me like a good friend. A pal. A buddy. I suppressed the urge to push him away and run down the hall. I knew my face must look flushed. I didn't care.

Another announcement for my flight echoed over the din of airport hustle. It was time to go. I turned to leave. To bid Elam farewell. My pulse had jumped to my ears in a rapid race. I wrapped my arms around him, and when he bent down to give me a brotherly peck goodbye, a surge of rebellion flooded all reason. I leaned into Elam and gave that kiss everything I had left. Elam jerked in surprise but gripped me tighter and kissed me back with a force that had my knees buckling. I couldn't stop and he didn't stop. We kissed for endless minutes, oblivious to the rush and buzz of everyone who passed by.

Frenzy gave way to reality. Elam eased back and averted his eyes. I saw him through the haze of tears that had filled mine. Time passed in slow motion as he stood there silent. I waited. Tell me not to go. Say something.

Nothing. His eyes had clouded. He opened his mouth to speak, but closed it again. The clock ticked. The woman on the intercom warned that it was the last boarding call.

I wiped my tears. "Goodbye, Elam."

He didn't call my name or try to stop me. My legs shook as I walked down the long hallway to the plane. We were in the apple orchard all over again. I didn't look back.

Chapter Seven

"He's really immature for a twenty-eight-year-old guy," said Joy.

The four of us sat at The Mason Jar that next Friday as I gave them sketchy details about my weekend—after they'd forced it out of me.

"He's not immature. He just doesn't love me." I laid my fork down. If I ate anything, I'd throw it up. "He never will."

Chrissy laid her hand over mine on the table. "I do not believe that. I know he feels more."

"You didn't see the beautiful Erin standing at his door at two o'clock in the morning. She volunteers at the same Boys and Girls Club. She gets to see him almost every day."

Elle grabbed a breadstick and bit down. "I would have told him how I felt the first day I got there,"

"I wish I had your courage sometimes, Elle."

"Gosh, I was only sounding brave because I'm frustrated. I'm not always courageous, as you well know. But Elam's been your best friend for eons. And you have the strength in you to do this. You have to muster it up. Go for the gold. Gird up your loins" she responded.

Joy jumped in. "I suggest she leave her loins out of it or it will make things much more complicated and confusing."

I actually laughed before more memories took me under. "You should have seen his legs in his bathing suit at the beach. They've turned into these amazing man-legs that almost gave my secret away because I couldn't stop staring at them."

Joy threw her hands up in the air. "Wasn't that the plan? To give your secret away and tell the guy you love him? For heaven's sake, give the secret away."

"Not like that."

Elle reached across the table and grabbed my hands in hers. "What are you waiting for, Holly? You want something more and I don't know what it is."

I looked at each sister through a haze of tears. "You are right about Elam and me being best friends, of course. And that's what scares me the most. He's seen me through some of the hardest times in my life and shared in all the fun—and crazy, too. One-sided love always changes things. And they almost never go back. I want my best friend for forever."

"But you want more than that, and you could have it. You could have it all," said Joy.

"But I risk losing it all."

"It's a risk you have to take or you'll go crazy, staying stuck where you are and never knowing. You love the guy too much to ever be truly happy unless you try for more," said Elle.

"If only he would try for more. I guess I want him to muster it up. I want him to want me so much, he comes running back here and grabs me like he did ten years ago. But this time he wouldn't let go."

All three of my sisters sighed and shook their heads in sympathy. Chrissy's eyes had teared up, too. "He will, Holly. He will."

\*\*\*\*

Elam sent messages, emails and texts about wanting to talk, that he wanted to explain, and about how much our friendship meant to him. "Friendship"— he'd used the friend-zone word in his message once again. I closed my eyes and fell back in my chair when I read that word, sure the floor had sunk beneath me.

And he didn't come to find me, to finish what could have started. We'd talked on the phone and texted for the last ten years. It never changed anything. If he wanted more, like I did, he would have stopped me from leaving or followed me back to Colorado.

After that first month, I could scarcely make myself play his messages or skim over his texts, and my responses were short and impersonal.

At the end of May I opened my laptop and clicked on Facebook. I'd kicked myself because I had avoided checking Elam's relationship status more thoroughly before I flew out to L.A. I went to his page to check for signs of anyone named Erin, and got sick to my stomach when I found her right away—a new post with a photo of the athletic blonde, Erin Casey with her arms wrapped around Elam's waist and the caption underneath, "The Two E's!"

I had my answer, my closure, my final break the minute I saw that picture of the two of them.

\*\*\*\*

I kept my jogging routine and willed the air to cleanse my body and my mind once and for all. Extra shifts at work kept me busy and focused on others. It helped. I met with my sisters at The Mason Jar and told them the subject of Elam Holmes was closed, over. Their eyes looked sad when I related the whole story.

Joy had been the only one to argue back. She pursed her lips before blurting out her frustration. "I don't believe it." She stabbed a chunk of cantaloupe with her fork. "A guy does not kiss you like he did at the airport unless he feels more than friendship."

Everyone nodded in agreement, but Elle's brows lowered. "Unless he's turned into some kind of player or a two-timer."

Chrissy jumped right in. "No way. We've all known Elam for too long. He's not a jerk. I think he has torn feelings or something weird is holding him back."

Elle shook her head. "Men change. And Holly deserves more."

Joy and Chrissy threw in their points and interpretations, and the three of them argued back in forth. I tried in vain to tune out their banter and stared blindly out the window while they tossed my heart around like volleyball.

"Elam's not a jerk," I finally projected into the storm of opinions. "Chrissy's right about that. We all know it. He just doesn't love me. Not enough or in that way anyway. He has his other E. And I have to let go. I mean, I have let go." I wiped at my eyes with my fingers and willed the vice grip around my chest to release. "Please."

They stared at me in silence. I leaned forward and rested my chin in my hands to keep it from quivering but my hands shook too.

"Well, I don't believe it's all said and done, but I think we need to respect your wishes, Holly," Chrissy finally said.

All three of my sisters gazed at me, their eyes open pools of empathy and love. I let the waves of tears flow down my face and the sob that had lodged in my throat broke free. Elle and Joy each grabbed one of my hands and Chrissy rubbed her hand on my back.

A few minutes later I blew my nose on the restaurant napkin and looked at my sisters through my puffy eyes. "Thank you. Now, can we change the subject to the hospital wing for Mom and Dad and Nicholas?

"Yes," they all chimed in together.

Chapter Eight

Our plans for the new pediatric wing at Memorial Hospital lifted my spirits more than anything else. The ground-breaking was only a few months away, and everything was falling into place. Contractors submitted bids, the committee planned a lovely ceremony, and Joy and Elle's kids talked excitedly about digging a hole for the "hopspiddle building", as Micah called it.

At long last I'd be somewhere close to my parents and baby brother every day.

I searched through family pictures and dozens of photos of Nicholas that would adorn the walls in the main foyer. We'd have a dedication ceremony and put up a plaque in their honor, too. The ache of missing them was balanced, at least a little, by the promise of happiness we'd all feel when this wonderful project our parents had started was complete.

The rooms would be full of children getting the love and medical care they needed and deserved. That was something we Frost sisters had insisted on—the whole wing would be known for its tender care of children.

I walked into the office of my boss, Carol, and told her I definitely wanted to work full time in that wing as soon as we had it finished and dedicated. She looked at me over the top of her reading glasses. "I have something even better in mind."

"You do?"

"Yes indeed." She stood up and extended her hand to shake mine. "I would like for you to be the head nurse of the entire wing."

I stared at her a few seconds to be sure she wasn't making a joke. Carol kept her hand extended and a smile on her face. I'd known her and worked here for six years now, but that was hardly enough experience to supervise a whole nursing crew. She must have seen the worry in my eyes.

"Shake my hand, Holly," she finally said. I shook it, my grip as weak as my shaking legs. Carol pointed at the chair behind me. "Now sit down and let me tell you why I want you in that position."

I sat straight down, grateful for the firm chair beneath me.

\*\*\*\*

"She told me no one would be nearly as devoted and invested in the care and success of that wing as I would," I explained to Chrissy when I stopped by her place after work.

She squealed in delight. "It's perfect, Holly! You will be amazing as head nurse of that wing, and we will be reassured that love and tenderness will always be there for the children."

The shakiness in my core was finally being replaced with tingles of happiness at the idea.

"But do you think I can really do it? I want everything to be so perfect."

"It will be—you will be wonderful at it, Holly."

"Well, my boss did say I could have all the assistance and staff I need to make it run smoothly."

"See." Chrissy's face glowed. "You're working it

out already." She jumped up and grabbed her phone. "We need an emergency trip to The Mason Jar so you can tell Joy and Elle in person—and celebrate."

"Agreed," I told her. My heart pumped with excitement. "Let's do it."

\*\*\*\*

Summer had arrived and the warmer air thawed my heart even more. I had accepted the job as head nurse at work, grateful I had time before the wing would be completed to study up and be ready to get things humming.

On the weekends, Mona Lisa and a bowl of popcorn kept me company while I watched movies, or Cara and Shelly and I hiked, or my sisters and I shopped for new clothes and books. I loved playing the role of "cool aunt" to my niece, Tatum and the boys at least once a week, too. Princess tea parties and ninja attacks on evil pirates always brightened my evenings.

\*\*\*\*

I worked a lot in the pediatric section, strengthened by the fact I would soon be able to help and maybe even save many children through the services offered in the new huge wing. I took medical classes in pediatric cardiology twice a week when summer sessions began. And I avoided Facebook—or at least a certain person on Facebook.

Life was good. Busy.

\*\*\*\*

Chrissy and I decided to hang out at my place one night, but she still didn't believe me when I said I was truly over Elam, and she tried to bring up the subject sometimes. I made her promise before she came that she wouldn't talk about him. We opted for doing our brows, having facials and painting our toenails, like we were teenagers again.

I lay on my bathroom rug with my head on a pillow in Chrissy's lap.

"Holly, for heaven's sake, will you please hold still?" she said.

"Y—ouch!" Haven't you tweezed enough by now? You're killing me."

"Seriously, we've done this a thousand times, and you fuss like this every time. You give people injections and draw blood every day, but you act like you're going to die when getting your eyebrows plucked."

"Plucked? You make me sound like a chicken."

"Maybe you are a chicken."

"Do you mean I'm afraid or I'm covered in fuzz?"

"Definitely afraid, or you'd call you-know-who back. Two more hairs and you won't be fuzzy anymore."

She finished and cleaned off my eyebrows with alcohol, and I decided to ignore her hint. I sat up with relief. "I swear you plucked ten times more this time. Maybe I'm growing hair like a Chia Pet."

"So, you're half chicken and half Chia Pet. I've believed that for a long time. Especially the first part."

I stood up and scowled at her. "Stop saying I'm afraid and stop hinting. I'll be dating around soon. I'm not calling Elam. He's with his other 'E'."

"Chicken." She smirked.

"Agh…" Sisters. Can't live with 'em or without 'em.

**\*\*\*\***

No more lecturing. I needed a good dose of kiddo

therapy. I called Elle to see if Tatum would like a trip to the toy store for a shopping spree. Holding Tatum's little hand, watching her eyes light up when we shopped or stopped at the bakery for treats, had always been one of my favorite activities. Elle had said yes, and I picked up Tatum on my way home from work.

After eating in the food court at the mall, I leaned across the table with a napkin and wiped cookie crumbs from her chubby cheeks. "Hey, baby girl, you want to pick out a movie to rent? And we can do each other's hair while we watch it?"

She jumped up from the table and clapped her hands. "Sure, Aunt Holly. Let's go!"

When Tatum picked the same movie for the third time, I told her we were done renting, and we stopped by the store and bought a copy. It was worth it—watching cartoon penguins fighting the bad guys once again. I had a growing shelf of kid's movies and craft supplies—as well as hair bows, Legos and Hot Wheels for Joy's boys, and crayons with a stack of white paper to transform into flowers, tic-tac-toe games, or airplanes. In nice weather, we took off to a park with a soccer ball. There was always plenty to do when the niece and rowdy little nephews came over to spend their "Aunt Holly" time.

We put on the penguin movie, and Tatum's hair slipped around my fingers like silk as I braided it. She smelled like powder and honeysuckle lotion. I imagined Elle's joy as a mother. Someday you'll be a mother, too, I'd tell myself.

As if Tatum could read my heart in those moments, she'd turn and look at me and climb up on my lap. Or wrap her little arms around my neck and press her puckered lips to my cheek. I would never grow tired of being an aunt.

Chapter Nine

A few weeks later a coworker introduced me to Jeremy, a very tan physical therapist who actually had a great personality under all that beefed-up muscle. We went out on a few "dinner and a movie" dates, and then he invited me to his family's condo at Rocky Point, Mexico. I jumped at the chance to escape.

The end of June the sea was warm, the color of deep jade, and full of sunbathers and water sports fanatics. Jeremy held my hand wherever we went, and I soaked up the trickle of comfort like a dehydrated sponge. The air hung heavy as the water, and the sun heated the sand until I swore I could hear it sizzle.

Jeremy almost had to shout to be heard over the screams of a group passing by on a banana boat. "This isn't the best time to bring you here. It's actually too hot and there are sting rays that come clear up to the shore. Slide your feet as you walk in the water and it will scare them away."

"Great!" I yelled in return. "Didn't you say your condo complex has a swimming pool?"

He laughed. "You can't come all the way to Mexico just to swim in a pool. This is the Sea of Cortez, where the edge of danger makes the whole trip more exciting."

I needed something to cool me off before the heat made me faint in front of a beach full of people. "Okay.

That makes sense." I gave him a thumbs-up to reinforce my resolve. "Let's swim with the stingrays."

Jeremy pulled me by the hand to the edge of the water, and I kicked at the sand as I entered to ward off any attackers—or stingers in this case. As soon as the water was deep enough, I pulled up my legs and waved my hands and arms back and forth under the surface to keep myself afloat and my feet above what I hoped was stingray level. A man rushed up beside us on a jet ski, making waves that slapped me in the face. I wiped at my eyes and spat a mouthful of salty water back into the ocean.

The man eyed me without apology, then turned his attention to Jeremy. "You wanna rent thees jet ski? Fifty dollards an hour. You keep two hours, eets only seventy-five dollards."

Jeremy grinned. "Sure, man. Let's do it."

The next thing I knew, I was flying across the top of the water behind him, my hair wild and tangling like a tattered flag in the wind. I closed my eyes, surprised at the exhilaration and freedom. I lay my head on Jeremy's back and tightened my arms around him as he pushed the Jet Ski to full throttle. I locked my fingers over Jeremy's six-pack. Maybe I could get used to this.

Refreshed and exhausted at the same time, we returned to shore and enjoyed a picnic lunch under the shade of a green-and-yellow-striped umbrella. Several people had set up camp on the beach and hung a king-sized sheet as a screen for anyone who wanted to join them for a movie. Jeremy and I brought our lounge chairs and watched *Pirates of the Caribbean* under the stars.

Before this trip, I'd never let him kiss me. Every

time I thought he might try, I found some reason to turn my head or hurry into my apartment.

Jeremy and I walked hand in hand at the edge of the water. The breeze cooled my skin and blew my hair back and forth over my shoulders like a caress. Jeremy's dark eyes searched mine and the moonlight glanced off his blond hair. He leaned down and kissed me, and I kissed him back. Nice. I'd take nice.

Nice went on for a while, and my confidence actually inched its way up the scale. Jeremy was the best guy I'd dated in a long time. There could be real potential here. People "moved on" all the time in movies and were able to love again. Elle and Joy were both single again, but not by their doing. There was no way those two wouldn't find love for a second time. Maybe, if I trained myself hard enough with Jeremy, I could, too.

**** 

"Train yourself hard enough?" responded Joy over the phone when I got home and told her my philosophy. "To fall in love? Sounds romantic; you make dating sound like boot camp."

I took a deep breath. "Well, it is in a way…you have to make it over obstacles and have determination and strength."

"Stop, you're making me swoon."

"Ugh. You know what I mean. Whoever said love—or even dating—is easy?"

"Whoever said you had to throw a grenade at your heart to get it to open? If it takes that much effort, is it even real?"

I choked back a sob in frustration. "Come on, Joy, I'm trying here. I might have to work hard for a while, but I believe I can do this. I can conquer my…heartache—I mean, my old memories—and get myself to try again."

She remained quiet, and then sniffled in the background, and I wanted to kick myself for bringing up heartache and having to move on again. She'd been devastated when Tom died in Afghanistan.

She inhaled deeply. "I know what you're trying to say, Holly. I've been there—I am there, or will be if I ever officially date someone. And I don't want it to sound like or be like I'm hacking my way through a jungle to make myself love again. Tom and I could talk about anything, and it kept the path open and flowing."

My tears flowed with her words. "Joy?" I managed to eke out without a sob.

Her voice grew soft and quiet. "Yes?"

"I have to do this…I have to believe I will be okay; that I won't always feel hopeless and empty."

"Okay, honey," she almost whispered. "Of course, you'll be okay, and you will love again. And I'll be right there beside you no matter what you need to do."

Chapter Ten

One evening at the beginning of August all three of my sisters stood at my door. My heart dropped to my feet and stayed there. "Did someone else die?"

Chrissy stepped forward and wrapped her arms around me, and panic tingled clear to my toes. Suspense did not work well in our family.

"Tell me now," I choked out.

Joy took a deep breath. "No one died, I promise. But we need to talk to you, anyway." She led the others through my front door, and we all filed into my living room.

"Okay. Out with it." I sat down and folded my arms.

Chrissy sat right next to me on the couch. "We all came because we have some news that might upset you." She squeezed my hand.

Elle sat forward, her eyes solemn. "I ran into Elam's mom, Dorothy Holmes. She told me that Elam is getting married."

I stared at the floor.

Elle took my other hand. "Did you hear me, Holly? Elam is getting married."

"I…uh…need to lie down."

Nobody moved, and my legs weighed a thousand pounds each, so I stayed where I was. All three sisters talked at once, but they were miles away. I picked up a few words here and there; for the better, didn't deserve, you'll be all right, call him.

"Holly?" Chrissy's voice dripped with sympathy.

Joy leaned in. "Holly, you look pale."

"Move over—let her lie down," said Elle. "Chrissy, get a wet wash cloth."

I lay on the couch and ignored the food, drinks and soothing words my sisters offered.

The next morning, I got up and went to work in a haze that wouldn't clear.

\*\*\*\*

It had been three weeks and I was still a zombie. Maybe I needed to let Jeremy off the hook. He didn't have to wait patiently while I decided whether I could ever feel anything again. I called him and gave him an abridged version of my history with Elam. He expressed disappointment and respectfully backed off. But sleep remained unattainable. Jeremy was a great guy. I liked him. I was definitely attracted to him. And he seemed genuinely into me. I questioned if I'd done the right thing and tossed and turned every night.

\*\*\*\*

September brought a crisp wind that curled and tinted the leaves on the trees orange, red and yellow. It took me days to notice. This is Joy's favorite season, and I knew she must be happy. But, fall always started the holiday season with Halloween, then Thanksgiving and finally Christmas. I kept a prayer in my heart that this year we'd find more of the joy our parents and Christmas had always given us.

My sisters and I met at The Mason Jar a few times. Joy and Elle did most of the talking and had stopped bringing up the subject of Elam. I sat back, relieved that they'd given me a reprieve from trying to cheer me up. Chrissy patted my hand a lot, so I knew my eyes must look as empty as I felt inside, but she didn't press me to talk about it. It gave me a chance to loosen the tourniquet that had wrapped itself around my lungs. At least with my sisters I could smile and make small remarks without having to think too hard.

On October first, I climbed out of my shell enough to notice the aroma of freshly lit fireplaces as I jogged. The sun sat low on the horizon and the evening chill seeped into the air. I reached into the pocket of my jacket and pulled out my gloves. One more lap around the park and I'd achieve my five-mile goal.

I slipped the gloves onto my hands, pushed myself to a full sprint and crossed the finish. My favorite part of running was right after I completed the last stretch. My blood always raced through every vein, and made my arms, legs and head tingly and light as a feather. I stretched and then lay back on the cold, damp grass of the park and stared up at the fading twilight.

The sound of an approaching vehicle brought me up on my elbows to be sure the driver looked harmless. A truck pulled into the parking lot, and as a man climbed out my ears started ringing. A long, lanky walk, well-worn Levi jacket, and thick, dark hair just long enough to bend the rules. The dizziness from the last lap I'd run took full control.

He walked over and stopped right in front of me. "It's good to see you, Holly."

I sat the rest of the way up, my thoughts spinning in circles over my head.

He stood there quietly, hands in the pockets of his jeans, exactly like he had at the airport months before.

"He…llo, Elam."

"It's good to see you." His smile looked forced and I braced myself.

I nodded. "Good to see you, too." I stood up and brushed off the back of my pants so he couldn't see my hands shaking. "What brings you to town?" Because I know it isn't me.

"I brought Erin to meet my parents."

The words slapped me in the face. The, "meet the parents" weekend, the laughter, the hugs of joy. All the things I would never have. I could hardly breathe.

"I heard about your engagement." I've got to get out of here before my chest explodes. "Congratulations."

"We're getting married in December."

Of course you are. That's when death occurs.

I pulled my keys from my pocket with a shaky hand and headed straight to my car. "I hope you'll be very happy." I yelled over my shoulder. I had to hurry away before the dizzy waves or the sobs of despair that climbed up my throat took over.

Before I could unlock the door, Elam grabbed my arm and pulled me around to face him. His fierce stare bore into me. "Wait a minute. I've tried to reach you and talk to you for months. We vowed to stay friends no matter what. Tell me what's wrong."

His eyes narrowed like they might cut right through me.

I gasped for air but my lungs wouldn't fill.. Maybe his eyes had sliced me open. "There's nothing wrong. And I'm…still your—"

"You cut me off like I didn't even exist, and I want to know why."

I stiffened. "I cut you off? I wasn't the one who stood there like a statue after we kissed at the airport." My voice shook worse than my hands. I hugged my arms in close and tried to catch a deep breath.

He let go of my arm and his eyes softened. "I know I reacted badly. But it wasn't a simple thing."

"I am and was well aware of your 'torn feelings,' Elam. But apparently, they weren't torn for long. You've moved on just fine."

"I called you. I wrote. I texted and I called some more. I knew you were upset, but you went dead cold toward me, and I want to know why."

My jaw locked tight. If I told him how shattered I'd been because he hadn't chased after me as I walked down the airport hallway, that he didn't chase me back to Colorado, I might fall to my knees and weep out loud. And what good would it do? He was almost a married man.

I took a calming breath and looked past him. "There is no big reason why. Life changes—one of us gets married and we just go on." I could not look at his face anymore and keep my composure while his intense scrutiny spread like fire on my skin.

"We don't 'just go on' and cut each other off after twenty years of friendship, Holly."

Friendship, the word coiled and constricted around my chest. I lifted my chin and kept my focus on the trees behind him. "Yes, we do."

He gripped me by both shoulders. "Look at me."

I did as he asked, but my eyes clouded. .

"I will not accept this. I am not giving up until you talk to me. You have to let me explain. I've wanted to for months." He held his hands out, palms up.

His pleading pricked my heart but it was too late for explanations that would only plunge deeper. I braced myself. "You need to get used to disappointment."

"I've had enough disappointment."

I exhaled in disgust. "You've had enough disappointment? From what? A few unanswered texts and phone calls from me? You haven't had enough attention from Erin to soothe and console you?"

"That's mean, Holly, and you know it."

I did know it. Tears burned behind my eyelids. I took a couple of deep breaths and looked into the face of the guy I'd known since third grade. The one who told me I was still pretty, even when my perms turned out frizzy in junior high. The one who held me for three days when my parents died.

His eyes remained steady, and the realization hit me: I'd been running away from his explanation—dodging his words, not wanting to hear him say once and for all that he didn't want me—that he didn't love me.

But I couldn't run forever. I was acting like a maniac. I had to face the truth. My adrenaline rush calmed down. "I'm sorry, Elam. Why don't you explain…"

Right in that moment his parents pulled into the parking lot and stopped across from my car. Erin climbed out of the back seat and started to hurry over to Elam but, stopped when she spotted me.

I looked with resignation into Elam's eyes. "There's your other 'E'."

I turned to walk away as Erin headed straight toward him, but he stepped in front of me, his brow furrowed.

"It's not that I don't care." He swallowed hard. "You know I do, Holly." Erin had almost reached us. "But I know it needs to be this way. It's best." His eyes brimmed with tears. "For everyone."

I had no time to let his words sink in before Erin arrived, an oversized smile on her face. "You must be Holly! How wonderful to meet you!"

"Hello, Erin," I answered, my voice pitched a little too high.

She stepped right between me and Elam, faced him, and landed a kiss right on his mouth.

I climbed into my car and drove away.

## Chapter Eleven

My car knew its way to the cemetery. My legs folded beneath me when I reached my parents' plot, and I sat down on the cold, damp grass. Oh Mom, Dad, how I wish I could feel your hugs and words of reassurance. I lay on my back and stared up at a finger-painted sky of royal blue and flecks of silver. Tears streamed down my face, the only warm spot on my body. After an hour I shivered so hard with cold I barely managed to hold my phone and call Chrissy. She answered and I sobbed. "I just saw Elam and I'm here at the cemetery."

She gasped. "I'll be right there."

Chrissy grabbed a blanket from the trunk of her car and wrapped it around me in a tight hug. She sat down next to me, near our parents' headstone, and I laid my head in her lap. It seemed so right to be here with at least one of my sisters. With our parents, and Nicholas or—close as we could get to them, anyway.

After several minutes my tears came back. "He's going to marry Erin. And I have to get out of here because I can't watch it."

Chrissy grunted in frustration. "You aren't going anywhere. This is your home. We sisters are your home. He can have his wedding and go."

" Do you know if he's moving back here?" I asked.

"I have no idea, but I sure hope not." Chrissy combed her fingers through my hair the way our mother used to always do. "Maybe we should send Joy and Elle over to scare him out of town."

"They could do it." I almost smiled at the thought.

"He'd run like a scared rabbit." Chrissy chuckled.

"He's a scared rabbit and I'm a chicken. What a nice pair we would've made. I guess he made the right decision after all."

"You don't really believe that."

"I don't believe anything anymore."

Chrissy pulled up a handful of grass and sprinkled it on my head and face. "Stop it. You know, Sis–I believe Mom and Dad are still close to us. I think they'd be sad to hear you say that."

I wiped the grass from my face and gripped some of the blades in my hand. "If I knew they could hear me, could see us, I think I could face anything. Mom would know what I should do."

She squeezed her hand over mine. "I think you know what she would tell you. You have to talk to Elam. At least you'll know you said all you needed to."

"I don't know what I'd say or where I'd get the strength."

"If there's one thing I've learned, the strength is already in you. You just have to find it and use it."

\*\*\*\*

I was right. Chrissy was wrong. I didn't have the strength. Elam and the other "E" left for L.A. a few days later. I knew because Joy and Elle had spied for me and seen them put their suitcases in a car and drive away.

I'd bought a gallon of ice cream, and for the next several nights I watched movies and let creamy chocolate soothe my wounded heart. When I emptied the carton I let Mona Lisa lick the inside. She, at least, had been my faithful partner, curled up on my lap and watching movie after movie with me. I was a cat lady.

My friend Shelly called me on Saturday and asked if I'd like to go shoe shopping. Sure, why not? I'm out of ice-cream anyway.

The sun shined like a new penny, and the air was so crisp and clean it snapped and crackled like fresh laundry blowing on a clothesline. The spark of energy lifted a layer of darkness.

I did love shoes. Shelly and I had gone on shoe sprees many times over the years. No other piece of clothing or jewelry could match that magical moment when a shoe slid onto your foot like a tailored glove. Like Cinderella and the glass slipper. But all my senses had dulled. The heady scent of soft leather usually intoxicated my senses the minute we entered the store. I always walked up and down aisles and viewed the displays like the royal jewels in London all over again. But now the displays seemed dull and scentless.

By the time we left the store, my face hurt from forcing a smile for Shelly, and I had three new pairs of shoes loaded in my bag. But I wasn't even sure which ones I bought. I got home and hoped Shelly hadn't noticed how weird I acted. Zombie movies and TV shows had dominated recent days, and I could fit right in as one of the main characters.

****

A week later Jeremy called and showed up at my house with a dozen roses. Red roses. He smelled good—manly and strong—and practically spouted poetry in an attempt to win me back.

"Holly, I don't know where I went wrong, but you

are beautiful as these roses and twice as sweet. Please go to dinner with me tomorrow night." He smiled like a little boy asking for a puppy. Puppies are sweet and cuddly. I nodded my head. "Sure. Dinner would be nice."

****

It was nice—lobster ravioli in butter sauce, artichoke hearts in the salad. Soft music. There was a dance floor, and Jeremy did have massive shoulders that were very comforting to lay my head on when the music slowed. And I was a total loser for giving him hope when I didn't have any. I felt good with Jeremy, safe and appreciated. And I'd been honest with him regarding the whole Elam history. Maybe I had to give our relationship a chance.

I had to admit it wasn't like a seventh-grade dance. At least not the dances I'd been to or agonized through with Elam. Later we watched a movie, and halfway through Jeremy stretched out his arm and pulled me against his side. I curled up and soaked in the comfort. A few minutes later he kissed me. I kissed him back.

He called me the next night and I agreed to pizza and bowling. Then walks in the park, a day hike in the mountains, and he even invited me over for dinner with his family. His mom embraced me at the door like a long-lost daughter. I blinked back tears.

I was all set to tell my sisters I was officially dating Jeremy again. The groundbreaking ceremony for the hospital wing was right around the corner and I couldn't wait. We had a lot to talk about.

Everything hit a bump in the road when I sat down at The Mason Jar and spotted a distinguished-looking man who walked in behind Joy. As he got closer, my heart jumped—this man looked like my father. Maybe Joy missed our dad so much she'd started dating an older man who resembled him. Before Joy had a chance to say much, I recognized the man as our father's brother, Simon, whom we hadn't seen since I was a young teenager. Of course, I knew he looked familiar. He'd always been nice to me and had performed silly magic tricks for us girls when we were young.

I was surprised to see him after—wow—at least fifteen years, but Chrissy jumped up and threw herself into Uncle Simon's arms. I wondered how she had recognized him so quickly, since she was a little kid when he'd suddenly disappeared from Colorado. My parents had never explained his departure, or even talked about him at all, as far as I could remember.

Uncle Simon gave Elle and me an awkward hug and sat with us explaining that he had been living out of the country for years, but was in the process of moving back to the Springs. I guessed he came back to find connections again—or maybe retire. It was a nice thing, I supposed. We were confused that he hadn't bothered to contact us when our parents died, but he explained it away by saying our family lawyer hadn't contacted him in Europe until weeks after the funeral.

He was inquisitive and warm, but after answering his questions about my career and marriage status, I had a hard time concentrating on the catch-up talk around the table.

Chrissy seemed entranced by Uncle Simon, and I was glad—maybe she could use the comfort of a loving uncle who looked like our dad.

The conversation ended up focused on the much-anticipated hospital wing, and I was happy to know everything was on schedule. November was around the corner, which meant the groundbreaking ceremony would soon be here. Uncle Simon promised he'd attend if he was in town, and after a few moments he hugged each of us sisters good-bye and sprinted off to a business meeting without ordering dinner.

He'd come and gone in a flash, but in any case, he'd asked to see us all again soon and exchanged phone numbers with Joy. Chrissy was especially happy about that.

My sister's and I finished our meals and as we walked to our cars, Elle lingered behind a moment. "How are you doing, Holly?"

"I'm doing pretty well now. I'm dating Jeremy again, and he's actually great. I think the future looks good."

She hugged me. "I'm sure it will be, for all of us."

\*\*\*\*

Jeremy wanted to go out almost every night, but I needed to pace myself for both of our sakes. November arrived and I invited all three nephews and Tatum over for a play night and sleepover the first weekend. They transformed my entire apartment into one huge fort—blankets and sheets made a tent over every piece of furniture and even suspended from a hook in the ceiling where I usually hung a plant.

I bought Nerf guns and a whole stock of Nerf darts for Hide-and-Go-seek. Charlie and Tatum played the aliens who searched for me and the twins, Mitchell and Micah, somewhere in the "fort." We exchanged fire and ran for cover until we all panted for breath.

When it got late we huddled inside the fort with a flashlight so I could read them silly little spooky stories.

Charlie convinced us all we had to sleep inside the fort on one big spread-out sleeping bag. Tatum curled up next to me and was the first to fall asleep. The twins nodded off with their legs sprawled crosswise over mine. Charlie looked at me when just the two of us were left awake. "Well, Aunt Holly, I guess the oldest ones are the last to fall asleep."

I smiled at him. A little man his daddy would be so proud of. "I'm awfully glad I have such a handsome guy to keep me company."

I thought my compliment would make him happy, but he frowned. "You are sorta pretty, so why don't you have a husband?"

I squirmed. "Thank you for saying I'm kinda pretty."

"But why? Why don't you have a husband? Don't you want one?"

My cheeks flushed. I'd put Jeremy off for over a week again. Charlie was still looking at me for an answer. "Sure, I want a husband. Someday. But right now I don't need a husband, and that's okay, too."

"It is? My mom wishes she still had my dad. I thought all ladies want to get married."

Pitiful—a seven-year-old could make you feel like your whole life was off track. I leaned over and mussed up Charlie's hair before I pulled him in for a hug. "Don't you worry about me, Charlie-boy. I bet you have lots of cute girls in your class at school, don't you?"

He smirked. "Yeah, I've got a couple girlfriends. But don't tell my mom."

Even my little nephew was luckier in love than me. The absurdity actually made me laugh out loud before I answered. "Those are some lucky girls to have you like them. Your secret is safe with me."

"Thanks." He lifted his brows. "But you better hurry and get a husband before you get too old."

I cleared my throat. "Oh, I will."

I couldn't even hide in a fort under a pile of kids. The truth appeared before me like a tortured ghost: Elam gets married next month. Elam gets married next month. No sweet dreams for Aunt Holly.

After Charlie dozed off, I opened my phone and clicked on Facebook. I looked up Elam's page, knowing I was a fool for doing so. I scrolled through his pictures and zoomed in on his eyes that had seen me go through the worst heartaches of life; that jaw line; the lips that had been mine for only brief moments in all the years I'd known him. I scrolled through the photos again and fell asleep curled up with the kids and my phone, the picture still open and zoomed in on Elam.

\*\*\*\*

Two days later I finished my shift at the hospital and headed to my car for the drive to the park. Even though I was beyond tired, I knew I needed a run to clear my head and shake off the doldrums. But when I rounded the corner I stopped in my tracks. Jeremy was on his way inside the hospital, riding in a wheel chair. I hurried over beside him as an aide pushed him into the emergency department.

"Jeremy, what happened?" I asked, and hurried to keep up with the rushing aide.

"Not sure," he managed. "But my side is killing me, and I've thrown up three times in the last hour."

"Oh my goodness. That might be appendicitis."

"Then someone get it outta there." He moaned and his head hung down.

Turns out I was right, and I waited in the surgical lobby until my friend Jill came out in her scrubs and told me Jeremy was in recovery. Since I was a nurse, I was allowed to go back early to be with him.

I grabbed a wet towel and wiped his face gently to ease any nausea as he woke up. His vitals looked good and color had seeped back into his tan face. He was handsome and nice, and especially patient. I'd given the poor guy the runaround, and looking at him sick in bed brought on a new flood of guilt. While he was still asleep, I leaned down and kissed him on the forehead.

"Maybe it was worth it," He mumbled, and his eyes fluttered open.

"You need to stay asleep and rest, young man."

He closed his eyes and smiled like a little boy faking sleep. "And you need to give me another kiss for comfort."

I chuckled. "How can you speak so coherently after all those drugs?"

"You have a way of waking up a man, Holly Frost."

I laughed again and sat in a chair beside him, holding his hand. It was my turn to be the patient and giving one.

****

I stayed in Jeremy's room that night to give him sips of water and watch over him. Time ticked by while he slept, and my head bobbed almost constantly. I'd worked a twelve-hour shift and exhaustion was catching up with me.

The stark white room grew cold. I was still in the

running clothes I'd changed into to catch a few miles on my way home from work. I wrapped myself in a blanket and kicked back in a recliner in the corner.

Jeremy tossed and turned in the familiar pattern of a patient in pain. I came out of my sleep to call the nurse. It took a while for the meds to kick in, so I sat in a chair beside him and held his hand until he could rest deeply.

The sound of voices woke me with a start. I was still beside Jeremy, with my hand clasped in his, and had fallen asleep with my head resting against the side of his bed. The room was bright, and someone stood on the other side of the bed peering down at me. I looked up into the face of my boss, Carol, and she smiled. "Looks like you are one devoted nurse, Holly Frost."

I pushed my hair out of my face, rubbed my eyes and stifled a yawn. "Oh no. Actually, I know this patient. He's kind of my boyfriend." I sounded like I was in high school. I sat up taller and a second person walked in and stood beside Carol. All the blood rushed from my head.

Carol held out her hand toward the man. "Holly, this actually works out nice. I want to introduce you to our Hospital Assistant Administrator for your new pediatric wing, Elam Holmes. I was just giving him a detailed tour. He'll be starting right before the groundbreaking ceremony, so he can be here every step of the way."

Thankfully, Jeremy was still groggy and oblivious to who was in the room. I rose slowly to my feet with my eyes locked on Elam. "You didn't tell me you were coming back. Or that you were applying at this hospital."

"I meant to tell you, but we got interrupted."

His words took a minute to sink in. "We've been interrupted a lot."

Jeremy started snoring. His IV still dripped, and the tiny line that peaked and dipped in the window of the heart monitor showed his healthy heart rhythm.

Elam glanced down at him and back at me, his face serious. "You didn't tell me you had a boyfriend."

Carol cleared her throat and looked back and forth at the two of us, her clipboard with the map of the hospital clasped in her hand. "Soooo, I take it you two know each other? Is this going to be a problem?"

"No." I walked over to the corner, grabbed my purse and then looked at Carol. "It's not going to be a problem at all." I glanced at Elam before I walked out the door, but I couldn't meet his eyes. "Good luck to you and your new job. You will be great."

He would be. He was going to be great at his job. A good husband—to someone else. A wonderful administrator. And my boss.

If my parents were my guardian angels, like so many people had assured me with sympathetic hugs at their funeral, then they were doing a terrible job.

**** 

Jeremy was released two days later, and I visited him at home like a dutiful "girlfriend." He was smiling and happy to see me, but I was starting to feel like a hypocrite. I'd tried to stir up more emotion—I'd wanted to feel everything. But my heart wouldn't let me, and at least I knew it wasn't only because of Elam. Jeremy and I were too different. And I couldn't use a nice guy like him for comfort. When I told him, he was disappointed, but I knew he'd be fine. He kissed me on the forehead before I left his house, and I hugged him a long time. Tears sprang up, but my feeling of loss went far beyond Jeremy. I turned and left without saying anything more.

I'd made another decision, too. One I'd have to tell Carol and my sisters about soon.

Life had shut many doors on me, but I knew a window would open somewhere.

Monday morning, I woke up feeling free. My new plan rose up like the sun, and I could breathe again.

Chapter Twelve

I was the queen of efficiency at work. Programmed, productive, smiling—until my cheeks hurt and my eyes locked straight at whatever or whomever I was working on. I didn't look around much, so I wouldn't see Elam, and didn't let my mind stray from my tasks. I finished my shift and checked my work emails. Carol had sent out notice for an impromptu staff meeting in the conference room. All employees finishing their shifts were asked to meet the new admin assistant, Elam Holmes. I snapped my laptop closed with a groan.

I waited until most of the room was full before I slipped in and took a chair in the back. Carol introduced Elam to the staff, and they all applauded. I clapped, too, and kept my eyes focused on the wall behind Elam's head so I could take in the information without being distracted by his eyes—or hair—or smile. I didn't need to learn any details about him, but I took copious notes on things I had known for twenty years to keep my hands busy.

I was fine if I didn't look at him, but the resonance of his voice slipped under my resolve. The depth and timbre I'd known and loved for so long made me doubt everything I'd planned to do.

Erin was there, sitting at the front as a special guest supporting her fiancé at his big introductory staff meeting. One glance at her threw cold water on the warmth from Elam's voice and sent me back to reality. I took more useless notes.

After the meeting, I tried to make my way out quickly, but one coworker after another grabbed me or stopped me to chat. Before I could escape, somebody had me by the elbow. I knew that grip, and was soon pulled to the side by Elam.

He wore an administrator's professional smile. "Well, Miss Frost, I look forward to working together."

"Maybe working together."

"Maybe? I was informed you were going to be head nurse over your family's hospital wing."

"It won't actually belong to my family. We're just supporting the foundation behind it and are part of the funds. And I'm thinking I may be too emotionally involved to do a good job as head nurse after all these years of ups and downs. I'm too close to the whole project because of my parents and brother and sisters. I can't let that get in the way of something that means so much to me."

His brow lowered. "You're totally contradicting yourself. What are you thinking, Holly? Your closeness to the project is exactly why you will be the best person for the job. No one else would give it half the care and investment that you would."

"I know a couple of nurses who would be fabulous. I'll give you or Carol their names."

"I don't want their names. I want you to do it."

"I appreciate your confidence…"

"Why are you being so formal?"

"We're discussing a pretty serious subject. Whoever does this job will have hundreds of children's lives in their hands."

"I'm more than aware of that. And I repeat: no one will do it as well as you."

"Thank you, Elam. I really mean it. But I won't be taking the job."

Chapter Thirteen

By the third week in November people were putting Christmas lights on their houses and covering their lawns with statues of reindeer and snowmen. Thanksgiving was only two days away, and the groundbreaking for the hospital wing was coming up on November thirtieth, in honor of little Nicholas' birthday.

Christmas was my favorite holiday as a little girl. We did all the wonderful family traditions: we shopped, shopped some more, baked, went Christmas caroling, and attended church. I hardly saw my mother without an apron through the whole holiday season. Music— jolly music rang and played day and night, and Mom hung a little Christmas bell over the door all through December. Every time people came into the house, they were met with a tinkling of seasonal cheer. Joy lives in our parent's house now, and she still puts the little bell on the front door. Warm memories gush, and then flood me with pain every time it rings. I use her back door in December.

Elam and I made a rule as kids that we could only give each other homemade gifts for Christmas. I knew his mom helped him sometimes because one year, when we were twelve, he gave me a stuffed teddy bear with a little bow on its ear. I named the bear Ellie in Elam's honor, and his face turned bright pink when I told him and kissed him on the cheek to thank him for it.

I made him cookies or a Christmas pie because, hey, he was a boy and my mom said they always like to eat. But after Elam gave me the teddy bear I tried my own hand at crafts and made him a wooden jewelry box from a kit I found at the hobby store. My dad helped me and showed me how to use a hammer and nail without hitting my thumb.

I knew Elam had the box for many years because he made a point to tell me anytime he added a keepsake. Things like ticket stubs from movies we went to together, old coins we found in our change, photo-booth pictures of us sticking our tongues out and making faces at the camera. I wondered if he still had it. I wondered if he'd keep it after he married Erin. There would be no more memorabilia from us to add.

I slogged my way through Thanksgiving and relished my time with my sisters and their kids. Joy invited a special man in her life to dinner this year, and Chrissy invited a friend of hers, too. They walked in the front door and the ringing bell clanged against my heart.

I could still eat turkey and pumpkin pie. Or any of the other six kinds of pie Elle made. But since our parents' accident, egg nog and nut cake made me nauseous. Each year was a little better, and I knew our parents would want us to feel the warmth and joy of our memories. We all worked hard to make Thanksgiving special.

This holiday season I would hear wedding bells ringing for "The Two E's." I'd hold my breath through that and the rest of Christmas, and then tell my sisters my plans to move and go on with my life. I was leaving

Colorado Springs for a brand-new start. I wasn't sure where I'd be headed, but knowing I didn't have to stay and see Elam married to someone else day after day, lifted the dark cloud that had covered my world.

****

November thirtieth—the ground-breaking day for the hospital wing had arrived at last.

I arrived early to help and to watch the workers set up the ceremony. I'd gazed at the empty field for months and months in anticipation of this—the day our whole family would feel all together again.

I placed large framed pictures of Nicholas and our parents on easels along the front of the crowd. Green astroturf covered a large area over the empty field, where dozens of chairs had been set up and filled with friends, professionals, and VIPs from the city.

My sisters arrived and we hugged each other and then hugged everyone we knew, giddy with excitement and happiness. I held hands with Joy's twins, and Tatum and Charlie marched beside us along the path where the new wing would be built. They all hopped and dashed around the area, and Charlie and Tatum chased Micah and Mitchell when they ran too far out of range.

The mayor was there, and all of the hospital administrators. I knew Elam would be in the crowd somewhere, so I kept my gaze moving and out of focus—all of my emotions were in high gear, and if I got too close and hugged him I was afraid I would burst into tears. .

Uncle Simon had come, looking handsome as ever and so like our dad. A quick flash of guilt hit me; he'd called the week before and asked if he could take me to lunch, but I was too busy. I'd have to make it up to him soon. It was so nice to have family here to support us. Our lawyer, Richard Arnett, had been by our sides from the time our parents had passed away and all through the plans for the hospital wing. He sat on the front row by the rest of us, like a surrogate father.

The sun broke through the November gloom, shooting rays of light on the crowd. My heart pounded and tears poured down my cheeks as the ceremony began.

The moment arrived and we gripped our shovels in our hands, ready to turn the first bits of soil over to signify the beginning of construction. We sisters grinned, cameras flashed, and we all froze in place when a man broke through the line waving papers in his hand—and ordering us to shut the project down.

The ceremony was cut off like the drop of a guillotine. People stood up in confusion after Mr. Arnett quickly perused the paperwork and then announced the ceremony would have to be postponed. I still held my shovel in my hand. Chrissy gasped, "Oh no," and the sun disappeared behind the clouds again.

The words whirled inside my head—a freeze on funds, a lawsuit, and a company called Lyonstone claiming rights. It knocked the wind out of me and I couldn't get it back. I'd sensed our parents and Nicholas near me this whole week, and especially today, but it all was slipping away.

****

My sisters and I sat side by side on leather chairs in our lawyer's office in a whirlwind of emotions while he read the "verdict" from the papers someone had filed against us. Our funds were frozen—everything looked alarmingly legal..

"It may even shut down the project forever. It could take months or years to figure this out, but I will put my full attention on it, I promise you girls. This is wholly unprecedented," said Mr. Arnett.

It hit all of us with a blow to the heart. Joy, Elle, Chrissy and I huddled together and cried, but then Joy encouraged us to keep our courage. We rallied then— we had to. The children's wing in our baby brother's name was so special, and wonderful. There had to be a mistake. We'd had the best professionals working on every aspect of the project.

We had to put our faith in Mr. Arnett, who promised us he would begin an investigation immediately and keep us posted. "Hopefully, we'll get things sorted out shortly after the New Year," he said. "Don't lose heart, girls."

I was the last to leave. I stepped out of the lawyer's office and stopped in surprise when Elam stood up in the lobby and came toward me. "Holly," he whispered.

Before he could finish speaking I fell against him. He wrapped his arms around me and led me into an empty meeting room. I sobbed out loud against his warm shoulder, for my mom, my dad, for little Nicholas and his hospital wing. And for the Elam I knew and loved, and had lost somewhere along the way. He rocked me back and forth in his arms and held his cheek against the top of my head.

After a few moments, I got control and stepped back. The front of his shirt was wet and smudged with mascara. "I owe you a new shirt."

"You don't owe me anything."

"You've seen me through a lot of tears, and I think

I owe you a medal of honor, not just a shirt." My voice broke and I fought the urge to burst into sobs again.

Elam tried to smile, but one corner of his mouth pulled down a little and his eyes were watery. "I owe you the world, Holly Francis Frost." His voice shook as he pulled me back in his arms.

Someone knocked on the door. In all of the emotion I'd forgotten that Chrissy had ridden with me and would wonder where I was. Her eyes opened wide when I opened the door and she realized I was with Elam. She spun around and headed back, but we'd both seen her.

"No, stay. Everything's all right," I mumbled as Elam released me from his warmth. "We need to go. Elam was just—"

"Call me—promise you will—if I can help in any way," Elam said. He touched my shoulder, nodded at Chrissy, and moved away. The door clicked behind him when he left and I grabbed Chrissy's hand.

I left with my sister, the scent of Elam's sandalwood soap haunting me all the way home. My plans to leave Colorado Springs seemed even wiser. I'd still help with our terrible mess over the hospital wing, but after that I had to breathe somewhere new.

## Chapter Fourteen

December First.

Noelle told me the wedding party for Elam's wedding had arrived in town. I couldn't leave my apartment or get into my car without fear that I might bump into one of them and have to put on a polite face.

I missed Elam's mom. We'd become so close over the years when Elam and I had been at either his house or mine all the time. She always wore the same big smile as Elam, and she had what she called laugh lines around her dark eyes. I'd seen her, more times than I could count, in their orchard working alongside her husband and children. I'd helped her make apple butter, apple sauce, apple cake and pie. She stood there awestruck as she looked at a new crop every year.

She and my mom had become friends, and even exchanged recipes and ingredients over the years. Mrs. Holmes attended my parents' funeral, and she'd held me while I wept. The past three years had been so desolate with Elam far away, and I'd only been to see his parents a few times. Now that he was going to marry Erin, I avoided bumping into his mom at all costs. All she'd have to do was look at me with her big, kind eyes, and I'd weep like a baby on her shoulder and reveal my whole heart.

Now I was playing dodgeball with the whole town of Colorado Springs to keep away from the Holmes family, and especially the "wedding party." I looked around every corner wherever I went. Seeing Elam would be hard, but seeing him with Erin would splinter the final fraction of my heart.

Chrissy had seen Erin at the bakery, oohing and awing over wedding cakes, and Elle had bumped into Erin and her mother at a shoe store. I had been glad Erin didn't know my sisters, so they wouldn't have to make small talk. But I should have known Elle would go out of her way to meet the bride, the reporter in her couldn't help it. She came over to my apartment after the shoe store encounter.

"Well, I just met the 'the fiancée' and her mother."

I grabbed my throat. "You did? How did you meet them? Was Elam with them?"

"Nope. I recognized Erin from looking her up on Facebook, and I wanted to see for myself what this girl is like."

I gulped. "And?"

"And she's pretty, but my lands, that girl cakes on the mascara and is skinny as a rail."

"That's it? She likes Mascara and has bony knees?"

She smiled at me in that "clever-eyed reporter" way of hers that always makes me panic. "I told her our family and Elam's were close friends, and she smiled and acted all happy to meet me. Then I told her how great Elam is—and that I was your sister, and the two of you had been inseparable growing up. She wasn't as friendly after that."

"Oh, Elle, you didn't."

"Oh, yes I did. I'm not going to sit back in silence. I was friendly and nice, so don't worry, Holly. I told the fiancée about my favorite memories of Elam and how close he's always been to our family and how we all thought the two of you would get married someday because you were always together."

I gasped. "Oh Elle, I never expected you to do that."

"Don't worry," Elle continued. "She smiled and nodded all tight-lipped while I talked, and her mother never said a word."

I covered my mouth to stifle another gasp and my heart sank. "I appreciate you being on my side, but it's not going to make a difference."

Elle leaned toward me on the couch. "It makes a difference in a very important way. It shows you, Holly, that you have a team who is on your side and that we sisters will be here for you all of our lives come what may. If it weren't for you sisters after my divorce and losing mom and dad, I never would have made it. Family is what lasts."

I hugged my big sister with a whole new strength. "You're right; we Frost sisters will last forever." I walked over and picked up my phone. "And now you have to call Joy and tell her what you did."

She smirked. "Joy will be scandalized that I was so bold."

"Huh, scandalized? Chrissy will be scandalized, but Joy would've been standing behind you today, poking you in the back to egg you on."

Elle guffawed. "Yes, Joy's ways are much more subtle than mine. But she still finds a way to kill the cat, even if she has to kill it with kindness."

I chuckled. "Yep. She may not have your boldness, but don't mess with her family."

I needed to laugh more than I'd realized. After Elle left, I fell asleep for three hours, the most rest I'd had in weeks.

Chapter Fifteen

December Twelfth.

I was a fool for driving down this road. Now that I'd turned on this one-way street, I'd have to pass by the church where Elam's wedding would take place in six days. I didn't even want to look at that building. Stupid, stupid move. And just as that thought passed through my mind, I came upon the dreaded place. Cars lined the parking lot, and an a-frame sign stood on the sidewalk with big black letters scribbled on white poster board, "The Two E's" Wedding Rehearsal." The words were arrows, piercing me right to my core. Rehearsal day—the first step toward my own personal D-day.

A familiar form with long blonde hair caught my eye—Erin. She walked out on the sidewalk in front of the church and spotted me the same instant I saw her. I jammed my foot on the brake in reflex, ready to back-up all the way down the street to get away. But before I could slam the gear into reverse, Erin came toward the road and waved me down. I forced myself to stay instead of tromping on the gas like I wanted to. The last person in the world I wanted to see was the blushing bride, but she walked right up to my car window, an overly bright smile on her face.

"Hey, Holly. We never got your rsvp, and we want to save you a special place real close to our table.

You're coming to the wedding, aren't you?"

I wanted to hate her heavily mascaraed eyes and skinny legs so bad in that moment, but the girl was actually nice.

"You're coming, right?" she repeated.

I almost choked. "Oh, I'm sorry. I'm going to have a family emergency next week. But I wish you the best. Well, I better go. Good luck." I turned the steering wheel to make a U-turn on the one-way road.

"Wait a minute, Erin. I'll talk to her." Elam had walked up behind Erin. I turned the wheels straight again and sighed in resignation.

Erin stood locked in place for several seconds before she glanced back and forth between me and Elam and then slowly walked away.

I stared straight ahead out the windshield instead of looking at Elam, and he leaned down and put his hands on my open window frame. "Why aren't you coming to the wedding, Holly?"

"Like I told Erin, I'll have a family emergency."

"You plan your emergencies?"

My cheeks lit on fire and I rubbed my hands over them. "It would be too—diffi…" Curse his sandalwood soap and the tears that leaked their way out of my eyes. I could easily reach out and touch Elam's hands as they gripped the window edge beside me. His nearness and my confusion combusted. I looked straight into his eyes and didn't care that mine were full of tears and he would figure out why. The dam broke. "Oh, forget the charade. You know why I'm not coming, Elam. You know why."

I slammed my foot down on the gas pedal, and he had to jump back as I screeched away.

I zoomed home and threw on my running clothes. I had to get rid of the horrible tension in my body before I lost my mind.

On my way to the park I had an impulse to drive by my father's office. I knew he wasn't there anymore, but the memories were, and I would take what I could get for solace. Instead of just driving by, I found myself pulling over in front of the tall, sleek building with huge, slanted windows.

The parking lot was empty. I got out, sat on the warm hood of my car and leaned back on the windshield. I closed my eyes. Within a few weeks I'd be out of here. The chill in the air matched the cold in my heart.

"This is where it all started."

I opened my eyes in shock to find Elam standing beside me. I took my time responding. "Go away."

"I'm not going away."

"Okay, fine. I'm the one going away. I'm leaving this place—you, the memories and the pain. You can have it all to yourself. I'm moving to Santa Fe as soon as the problem with that stupid Lyonstone Company is resolved and a new groundbreaking date is set."

"You don't need to leave because of me."

"Don't I?" I tried to laugh, but it came out as a grunt. "I've come to realize that you have a nasty habit of sneaking up on me."

"Sorry if I startled you."

I sat up, puzzled. "This was my father's office building. What did you mean, 'This is where it all started'?"

He put his hands in his pockets and took a good long look at the office before he spoke. "Because something started here—and some things actually turn the tides of destiny. This is where one of those tides changed."

"My dad's business? A 'tide turner'? What on earth are you talking about?" I asked.

"A tide change, or at least a course change that brought up a wall between you and me."

I pressed my palms against my eyes to ease a pulsing pain. "You are not making one bit of sense, and if I'm not mistaken, you are late for your wedding rehearsal."

"We are already finished."

I lowered my hands but wouldn't look at him. "Then I'd bet Erin is wondering where you are. You best be on your way."

He leaned back against my car as if he had all the time in the world, his jeans worn thin where he kept his wallet in his pocket and his leather jacket open in spite of the cold. His unruly hair had been tamed into a nice, trim, administrator's cut; so strange, grown up, real. No longer the boy I'd loved, but the man I....I took a drink from my water bottle and pressed my fingers over the flush in my cheeks.

Elam always needed a haircut. It was one of those tasks he forgot about, like getting his tires rotated or his oil changed. It gave him a tattered look. No, it gave him a rugged look. Like a school teacher who would take his class on a safari or out on a survival quest. An impulse to lean into him for comfort zinged through me. Agh, I'd never win this tug of war. Time to retreat.

A few minutes passed in silence, and even with my ripped-up emotions, having Elam so close to me actually calmed me down. He finally spoke. "Why are you here in front of your dad's business?"

"I come here sometimes when I want to feel close to him. Even though strangers bought it a couple of years ago, this place still reminds me of him."

"It could have been me."

"What? Who could have been you?"

"The buyer. If I'd taken a certain offer, it might've been me who took over your father's business."

"You, an aerospace engineer? I never imagined that suited you."

"That isn't what your father believed—or maybe wanted for his daughter."

"Wanted for his daughter? Elam, you're talking in bits and pieces. I've been crying, my head aches and I can't think straight." Chills shook me clear to the bone and I wrapped my arms around my body to preserve what little warmth I had left.

"Okay, I'll explain. But I'm going to tell you the whole story. And then we can talk about why you've been crying."

I ignored the second part of his plan. I had no desire to discuss my tears with Elam when he was the cause of them. I lowered my brow. "You have, 'a whole story' about my dad's business? Something I don't already know?"

He nodded his head, and his eyes grew dark and serious.

I sat up straighter on the car. "Okay, I guess you'd better tell me."

He looked up at the sky and hesitated for a moment as if dreading the mysterious story.

I took a breath through my mouth because my nose was plugged from crying. "Elam, it's me. Go ahead and tell me what you're talking about."

He scooted closer beside me. "When I was seventeen, during our senior year, your father called and asked me to come to his office for a talk."

"He did? What on earth for, and why didn't you ever tell me?"

He pressed his finger onto my lips to quiet me. "Shh—I said I'll tell you the whole story. I went to your father's office when he called. He was real friendly and patted me on the back. I remember he gave me a tour of the building and then showed me all of the pictures and golf trophies he had around the room.

"I wanted to ask him why he needed to talk to me, but after a few minutes he jumped in; I remember his words like it was yesterday. 'Elam, I've noticed the way you look at Holly, and I can guess how you feel about her. And I would venture to guess that she feels the same about you, too.' I almost gasped out loud in surprise. He'd seen right through my nonchalant act. And I was even more shocked that he thought you might have feelings for me too. But your dad said it like it was an obvious truth, and with that air of strength he always had, I didn't question him or argue."

Elam's words made no sense. "My father talked to you…about feelings for me? Neither you or my father ever hinted that you talked about anything. Especially me and feelings of any kind."

"Hold on. Let me tell you the whole story. Then your dad started on comments like, 'I don't know what your plans are for your future…I'd like to take you under my wing…let's make a successful man out of you,' and so on. I think he would've made a good sports coach."

Elam smiled, but his eyes stayed serious. "He talked about you too. Comments like: 'We've always tried to give Holly the best...you'll want her to respect you as a man...you need a thriving income...you two come from different worlds...success is something we can do together....And the clincher—'I want to help you be all that you can be.' A whole narration followed about how he wanted to help me be successful."

I gulped, sure that my face looked bright red. "Oh, my gosh, Elam. I can't believe it. I never ever told my dad you had feelings like that for me. And as for the other part, I know he always loved you and talked about how smart you were, and that you were such a hard worker."

"He was watching out for his daughter. He told me he was sure I had potential, that he knew my family did not have much money—and I knew he meant money like you had grown up with, and he wanted to 'sponsor my education.' But I read between the lines; I wanted to be a school teacher at the time, and I told him so. It's a noble career, but the money is a lot less than a successful aerospace engineer's. Once his words sank in, I took them to mean that a school teacher would never be enough for you, but most of all I realized I would never be enough for you."

I jumped off the hood of my car and grabbed onto Elam's arm. "Elam, that is not true. Why would you believe such a thing?"

"I was seventeen and too self-conscious at the time. Your dad was a superhero to me."

My chest ached. "My dad was wonderful and a great engineer, but he wasn't always the best with words."

Elam half shrugged. "Like I said, I think he was just trying to look out for his daughter."

The realization that my father's intentions had caused Elam pain hurt me. Here came another wall of tears.

Elam cupped my face in his hand. "Holly, the last thing I want to do is stir up pain over your father."

I looked deep into his eyes. "I'm so sorry it came out that way, Elam. I don't know if you know this, but my dad sponsored almost a dozen students in college with scholarships and gifts. He kept it on the down-low, but he loved taking young people under his wing—and with no pay back. He'd always tell them to pay it forward."

How I wished I could run into the building, find my father and have him explain it all to Elam the right way. "My dad loved and admired you."

"I had no idea that was what he meant. I was a kid. A kid with a humble upbringing who took what he said in all the wrong ways. I knew you'd grown up with a certain lifestyle, the top of the line and even luxury. You were diamonds, silk and fashion. I was Levi's and pick-up trucks. I knew I could never be like your dad, and you adored him. I believed you'd want someone like him."

"But you are like him, in so many ways."

"I had to see who I was for myself." he said. "And I could never keep you from your dreams. I went back and told your dad that I knew my path was in education, in teaching and I appreciated the offer but I wanted to pave my own way. We shook hands, but he didn't smile like he had before, and I took it that he was disappointed in me and my plans."

My pulse pounded in my ears. I had to interrupt him. "I love and miss my father every day, but he was not perfect. He obviously didn't explain himself well to you, and then he misunderstood your response. I am so sorry it came out that way, Elam. Your family is amazing."

He smiled. "Well, I appreciate that, Holly-wood. I love my family. And now I see your dad's words from a whole new perspective. He invited me to his office again when I came home after my first year of college. He tried to change my mind and get me to accept his sponsorship, so to speak; he even mentioned that I might want to come into his business and take it over for him someday. He was warm and cordial, as always, and he sounded like he admired my desire to be a teacher, but I left there even more convinced that he believed my vocation would never be good enough for you. Now I see that was all in my head."

I sighed. "Why didn't you ever tell me any of this?"

"You were dating Sam Owens again by then, and I remembered how you'd chosen him over me in high school. Sam seemed more like the engineer type— someone who could carry on your dad's business. Things seemed doomed between you and me, as far as anything romantic, at least. I respected your dad. I stepped back, thinking he'd prefer someone more like Sam for you.

"I went back to college and spent months trying to prepare myself for you to marry Sam. And then I convinced myself that Sarah could make me forget my feelings for you."

I grasped my throat with my hand and swallowed.

"Why didn't you ever ask what I felt or wanted?"

"I never meant to make any decisions for you, but right then you were seriously dating Sam. What was I supposed to do—take you aside and ask you if you'd like to leave the 'most-likely-to-succeed-guy and step down to my level instead? I also respected your father and could see what he had envisioned for you in Sam. I didn't want to cause problems between any of you." Elam hesitated and looked at me with softness in his eyes. "And then, when your parents died, Holly, I felt honor-bound to let your father's dreams for you come true."

I fell against Elam's shoulder and burst into tears. He put his arms around me and I gave way to a whole flood of emotions I couldn't express with words. Strength emanated from him and soaked through my skin clear to my core. The chill I had let overwhelm me melted away. I closed my eyes to drink it in for the few moments I could, but ultimately, I was in the arms of someone else's fiancé. I pulled myself together and eased my way out of his arms. It took me a minute to speak again, and when I did, I'd cried so much I sounded like I had a terrible cold.

"My parents died almost four years ago. You've had so many chances to tell me this whole story."

"The things your dad told me he wanted for you were like a part of his legacy when he passed away. I decided I had to keep things to myself, let you go and move on in order for it to happen."

His words pressed down like the storm clouds that gathered and hung overhead.

I remembered how I'd kissed him so passionately at the airport, when all along he'd decided to keep away from me. My face burned in humiliation.

But he had kissed me back. And he hadn't been able to hold back the intensity, either.

I took a deep breath. "If you were living by these beliefs, Elam, then why did you kiss me back at the airport last May?"

"I'd wanted to kiss you like that since the time in the apple orchard after high school. I gave in and I couldn't stop."

"So, just unfulfilled desire or the heat of the moment got the best of you?"

"No. You know it was more than that."

"Do I? How am I supposed to know that? I feel like I haven't known the truth for years." I didn't like the anger now bubbling up in me, but I couldn't stop it. I was angry at both of us.

"What do you think I was trying to tell you in all those phone calls, messages and emails after you flew home?" he said defensively. "I was going to tell you the whole story about the talks with your dad and why I'd moved on after the accident. After we kissed, like that, I knew I couldn't deny how I felt about you. But it was complicated."

"Complicated? It seems pretty clear to me. I've been an oblivious fool. I threw myself at you, and all along you had made a firm decision to—to let me go and live behind walls I didn't even know existed. I've had no say in my own life at all and I didn't even know it."

He held me by the shoulders. "Wait, Holly. Just stop for a minute. I wanted you more than anything or anyone in the world, for years. But before you came to see me, I had tried to move on and I'd asked Erin to marry me. We had some troubles after that, and she hadn't answered yet, but I'd asked her. She knew about my torn feelings for you and of course she resented it. We were trying to work it out before you flew back to see me. I was a selfish idiot to kiss you at the airport before you left, but…" His eyes filled with tears. "But I had to. I had to at least have that much before I let you go."

"And that was enough? You could go on and marry someone else after that?"

"No. After we kissed I didn't want to marry Erin. I wanted you. But my old doubts and that honor for your father still hung over me. I wanted to talk to you about it so you could understand, and because I wanted to know if you had feelings for me beyond the attraction, but no matter how I tried to contact you, you would never answer me."

The moment came, I had to ask the most painful question of all. My throat tightened. "If you felt so much, why didn't you come after me?"

"I finally did. I flew back here to tell you everything, but you were gone. You were in Mexico with Jeremy. I thought I had my answer so I flew back to L.A."

I covered my face with my hands. Elam had come for me. He'd tried to tell me everything. I'd had a chance to have it all, and I'd been a distant, stubborn fool. I looked into his eyes and realization dropped like an anvil in my stomach. "And when you got back to L.A, Erin said yes to your proposal, didn't she? And now you're going to marry her."

He nodded his head solemnly. "Yes."

I'd lost him. I'd come so close and lost him. I

stepped away, my head spinning. I wanted to crawl into a hole and die. "I've got to go."

"Holly, wait." He took hold of my arm. "I'm sorry."

My chest heaved, and I knew I was going to hyperventilate. I pulled my arm away. "I can't. I can't do this or take this anymore. I've got to go."

Chapter Sixteen

I made it to the park as the clouds gave way and a deluge of rain poured from the sky. I climbed out of my car and took off at a run down the path around the greenbelt. Elam's words repeated over and over in my head and pelted me harder than the freezing raindrops. His wedding was only days away. My stubborn pride had cost me everything. I picked up my pace, willing the warmth in my calves to take over the rest of my body. I pumped my arms as icy drops the size of quarters soaked through my jacket and hair. Wind whistled through the tall pines that surrounded the park. Rain and tears blurred my vision.

After years of heartache, I'd actually had a chance with Elam. And now, in a few days, he would marry another woman and disappear from my life, like he'd never existed. Emptiness blew through me like the wind through the trees, and I could not stay rooted in place and take it. My father had tried to help my life, but the whole plan had backfired. Elam had cut off his feelings for me to please my dad. I had cut Elam off and we'd both tried to bury our feelings in someone else, over and over.

"Agh," I shouted into the unfeeling rain. "No, no, no!" Now that I knew how huge those mistakes had all been, it was too late.

The track around the park spun in circles. I gritted

my teeth and took off through the forest at a full sprint. Branches slapped my cheeks as I pushed past trees and bushes. I would pack, leave, get away from here and never come back—even before the holidays. I would run until I found a place where I would never have to see Elam as a married man.

I came upon a creek with a wooden bridge. My joints ached and had stiffened in the cold until I worried I might stumble. I ran to the bridge and crawled beneath it on one end. Water gushed over huge rocks in the creek a few feet in front of me, while rivulets seeped through the cracks between the wooden planks overhead and dripped down my neck. There was no place to escape it, and the wind chill bit through my soaked clothes. I cupped my hands and tried to breathe warmth into them, but I could hardly get my breath. My throat burned like fire but the rest of me shivered out of control.

I remembered a thin rain poncho packet I kept in an inside pocket of my jacket. All my emotions had jumbled my common sense. I slipped the poncho on and felt a measure of relief from the wind and dripping rain. I huddled into a tight ball and tried to calm down.

Over an hour had passed since I'd climbed under the bridge but the rain hadn't stopped, I hadn't really warmed and there was no calming down. I'd be in trouble soon if I didn't get warm. The temperature would drop rapidly with the sun.

When I crawled out from under the bridge, the rain had turned to sleet that stung my hands and face. I'd been crazy to take off into the forest in December during a storm. By morning the land would be covered by ice and snow. I'd run fast for a long time and with no sense of place or direction. The sky had turned such a dark gray I couldn't be sure where the sun was setting. Fear welled up again, but I pushed it back. I had to stay in control if I was going to find my way home.

After jogging in three different directions I ended up back at the bridge over the creek again. I had to face the facts; I was lost. Deeply lost. I said a silent prayer as panic tried to take my reason.

I huddled beneath the bridge to think. I'd seen a movie once where a lost person covered himself with leaves for a blanket. I looked out at the soggy ground. Dripping leaves would do me no good. I couldn't build a slushy ice cave. I had nothing to use to cut branches to make a lean-to against the bridge. I had a crazy fleeting regret that I'd never joined the Girl Scouts as my mom had wanted me to as a girl. I was helpless as a child out here. My medical training helped me know what my body needed to survive, but I had no idea how to get it.

Dusk moved in like a dark shadow. The sleet slowed but didn't stop and the wind howled like wolves on the prowl. I gave in to my fears and even cried out for help, although I knew no one would hear me in this storm.

Panic spread over my body, and I shivered and curled into a ball close to the ground.

"You have a nasty habit of running away," said a familiar voice.

I lifted my head quickly and squinted past bright lights and shooting ice drops into the glorious face of Elam Holmes.

A dog barked nonstop next to him, and the beams from his ATV blinded my eyes. Elam helped me crawl from beneath the bridge, wrapped a blanket around me and guided me to the ATV. He climbed on and I got on behind him, huddled up against his back. I couldn't stop shivering, and an irrational fear entered my mind that I would freeze to death before he got me to safety. His dog jumped up in a basket on the fender. Elam turned his head. "Now hold on. And no running off while I'm trying to drive."

I held on with numbed hands and fingers and nestled my face against him. His jacket was wet, but his warmth permeated through it. We made it to my car, my teeth chattering so hard I couldn't speak at all. He helped me into the passenger seat, dug the keys from my frozen jacket pocket, and invited his dog into the back.

After he drove me home, Elam went straight to my bedroom, grabbed my flannel pajamas and robe from my room, and then turned on my shower. "Can you get your clothes off okay?" he asked.

"Yes," I mumbled.

He smiled. "Oh. Well, all right. Go get warm, then." He nodded. "I want to talk to you when you're finished. I'll make some hot chocolate."

I did as he said without arguing but had no desire to talk about our doomed history and future anymore.

After I'd showered and dressed, he gave me a cup of cocoa and wrapped me in two blankets on the couch.

He sat down on the other end and smiled while shaking his head. "You know, the first time I spotted you up in that tree in third grade, I just had to climb up there to sit beside you. And right now, I'm not sure if that was the best decision or the worst mistake I ever made in my life."

My foolish behavior running off in the forest flashed before me again. I set the cocoa down and pulled the blankets over my head.

Elam tugged the blankets back. "No more running or hiding for either of us, Holly-wood. We're figuring this whole mess out once and for all."

I kept my arms wrapped tight around my knees. "I thought we had done that."

He signaled me to take another swig of hot chocolate before he continued. "Not yet so hold on."

He drank from his own cup, slow gulps like he was thinking and enjoying taking his time. Slow gulps that made his jaw muscles flex. I sighed in exasperation. "Thank you so much for coming to help me. It's getting late now. Is there that much more you need to say?"

"Ok, I'll get on with it. And if you'll bear with me, I'd like to start at the beginning."

I nodded and he sat his cup on the coffee table.

"Until I met you, all I cared about was climbing trees and fishing and getting into mischief. You liked that stuff, too, so life moved along just fine, until you grew into a full-fledged girl and cast a spell on me I couldn't shake. And it hasn't always been easy.

I figured out where I stood when you picked Sam over me in high school. I believed I had my answer, something I had to get used to. I understood I wasn't going to win your heart, no matter how many hours we'd spent climbing trees and getting ice cream or listening to your Brittney Spears CDs."

I smiled at the memories in spite of the painful part of his story.

Elam paused for a minute and smiled back at me. "I still can't believe you got me to wear that wig and halter top for the lip-syncing contest junior year."

We both chuckled, and in spite of my frustrations I wanted to toss the blankets off and throw myself into his arms.

Elam narrowed his eyes as if he could read my mind. "Okay, so we have this intense attraction between us. And it got the best of me more than once over the years. Each time it happened, I believed I had to get away from you fast before I caused a rift between us or you and your dad.

But I'm not an insecure kid anymore. I'm not even a clueless college student. I know who I am, and I know what I want."

He turned to face me. "I've never been okay without you, Holly.. I've been happy with my path in life, and I thought it was right for me, but even when I was with Erin, I was hollow without you."

My eyes widened. "What do you mean, when you 'were' with Erin?"

"After you and I talked in front of your dad's office earlier, I knew what I had to do. I went back to see Erin to call everything off. But before I could even say anything, she said she needed to talk to me. Like I said, I'd told her about our relationship and my torn feelings all along. Things were rough sometimes, and we almost broke off our relationship over you several times."

I inhaled so fast I coughed. All this time I'd believed he was on a perfect cloud with Erin and had nothing more than an unwanted attraction for me.

Elam kept on with the story. "Erin told me she saw the whole picture in just the few moments in front of the church today, when I walked up to your car. She realized how much there was between us, more than I'd been able to admit in ten years. She decided she wanted more than the half of me I could give, and she broke up with me."

"She did?" I could barely breathe. "You don't even seem that upset about it."

"I'm sad and guilty over the pain and confusion I put her through. She's a good person and didn't deserve any of that. But she was right. I didn't truly love her. I mean, not in the way love is meant to be."

Hope tried to climb its way to the surface but I was too scared to let it out until Elam finished. I interlaced my fingers together to keep them still.

"I went to the park after I talked to Erin. I wanted to find you right away and be totally honest once and for all. I guessed you'd go running to combat your feelings again. I found your car with your phone in it, but I couldn't find you. The rain turned to sleet, and I got worried, so I went back to my parents' house and got my dad's hunting dog and ATV to try to track you down."

He looked at me with a deep frown. "And it's a good thing I did. You might have frozen to death out there."

"I was going to find my way back." I lied.

"You were utterly lost, so admit it."

"Yes, I was lost. I admit it. You happy now?"

"Not even remotely."

I sighed. "What do you mean?"

"Because of this craziness between us. Every time I've decided to open up or make a big move, you've run away or cut me off and ignored me."

I pulled the blankets over my head again but then yanked them back down to glare at Elam. "Wait a minute. You can't put this all on me. You'd kiss me like you meant it, but then you'd run off or just stand there while I left."

"Well, now you know there was a lot more to the story. I did fly here to find you, Holly. I wanted and tried to talk to you for weeks and months."

I swallowed hard and closed my eyes. "I've wanted to tell you how I really feel for years, Elam. For years." I opened my eyes and looked right into his. "When you picked Sarah in high school and stayed with her for so long, I was lost on the inside, or adrift or whatever lonely metaphor you want to use."

My head ached from the exposure to the cold and the mixed emotions that pounded me. I just wanted to be surrounded by Elam's arms, and stop all this talking. But I kept on. "You stayed with her and dated her for so long, I was sure I'd lost you forever. I kept moving and kept dating, to try and find happiness or fill this horrible void.

"And then when my parents died, and you came running, I let my guard down. I couldn't have survived it without you. I think I crawled inside your arms and your soul in those three days." I wiped at the tears that began to flood down my face. "I knew you had to go back to school, but I couldn't even let myself think of who else would be waiting for you. I was too devastated already."

Elam grabbed the tissues off the coffee table and wiped my tears. He pressed his palm against my cheek. "I loved your parents, too. They were wonderful people. And after spending those days with you, when I got back to school, I broke it off with Sarah."

I nodded, drinking in the touch of his hand, but the

memory of him walking out the door to talk with Erin when I visited in April popped up like a bad dream. I sniffed and tilted my head back against the couch, away from his hand. "I remember how relieved I was when you ended things with Sarah. And I'm not blaming you for all this mess; I've sent you wrong messages, and my dad made things even more complicated. But I'm through with the half stories. I want you to know the truth, and not only the parts I've let myself admit to you."

"Then tell me why you pulled away from my hand just now," he said.

"Because there are some things that still hurt so much. I pull away to protect myself when I think about them. I've done that for years."

"Which things?"

I did not want to relive the memory again, but I had no choice. I took a deep breath. "Elam, when you got together with Erin, right in front of me last April, a part of me died. I decided to give you up completely. I gave you every ounce of strength I had left when I kissed you at the airport. And when you kissed me back, I couldn't help but have at least a little bit of hope, even against my will. I came back to Colorado aching for you to come after me—to feel something, anything, for me. But you stayed behind, and I was devastated.

When my phone rang or a text or email came from you, I knew I couldn't take the disappointment anymore. I knew you couldn't feel even a grain of what I did for you, or you would have come running back here to fight for me. After a while I couldn't make myself look at your messages or listen to your voice."

Elam leaned closer, his eyes deep and somber. "I

am so sorry, Holly. So very sorry. I should have come for you sooner. I waited too long and made wrong choices. I've cared for years and wanted you so much without letting it show, even more than I could admit to myself. I hope you understand why I've been such a fool. It seems so ridiculous and so obvious now. I was blind and stupid. Even scared."

He took my hands and held them tightly. "But I'm not blind or scared anymore. So hear me now; the biggest and most important secret I've kept from myself and you is that I love you, Holly Frances Frost. I know that more than I've known anything else in my entire life. I love you and I want to spend the rest of my life with you. Only you."

He pulled me closer, took my face in his hands and rubbed his fingers across my cheeks where the tears had left their trails. "I've loved you since I climbed that tree in third grade and took a look into these beautiful eyes. And I want to know how you feel about that, and me, with no looking back...and before you try to run off again."

I laughed through my tears as joy overtook all reason. I couldn't talk past the knot in my throat. I couldn't form words into a sentence. I finally blurted, "I love you, too, Elam," right before his incredible mouth got the best of me once and for all, and we plunged into a kiss.

Pain melted away in a tide of warmth, and I wrapped my arms around his neck, my blankets making a cocoon around us as one kiss led to another. His whiskers softly scuffed at my chin, his hands glided over my back, and his lips held the faint flavor of honeyed apples.

I somehow knew my parents could feel my happiness as the dark cloud over the month of December lifted, and the echo of joyful Christmas bells rang in the distance.

I'd asked the angels a hundred times why they made Elam's lips so perfect, but I didn't have to ask them anymore. They made them just for me.

To conclude the story of the Frost sisters with the fourth book of the series, you'll want to read...

# Chrissy's Catch

## by

## Jeanie R. Davis

It begins like this:

Chapter One

Gasping for air, I clutched the counter-top while everything spun out of control. "I can't breathe! I'm going to die!" My chest constricted, and my heart pounded, echoing in my ears.

"Chrissy, what's going on?" My sister's voice on speakerphone snapped me from the attack. I gulped air like a parched camel guzzling water. Of all people to have heard me freak out, it had to be my over-protective sister Elle.

I hadn't had an anxiety attack in months. I looked

around for a trigger. Aha! My eyes landed on a new note from my roommate. She rarely left notes, her messages generally came in texts. Her handwriting, so eerily close to my late mother's, must have set me off. Elle couldn't find out—she'd have me committed.

"Chrissy! I'm coming over there!"

"No! I mean, sorry, Elle." I infused my voice with cheery optimism and forced a laugh. "I saw the cutest guy walk past my window. Uh...he took my breath away. Thought I might die." I rolled my eyes at my corniness.

"Now I know something's up. Since when do you get all gaga over a guy?"

Noelle was right. Years had passed since I'd opened my heart to a man. I'd had casual flirtations, but nothing serious. What had happened? Did I not trust them? Or was it me I didn't trust?

"Chrissy?"

"I—I guess you had to be there. Anyway, I'm fine. What were you saying?"

Dashing to the bathroom, I splashed water on my face, closed my eyes and took three long breaths. *You've got this, Chrissy*, I told myself, shrugging off the attack. My pale reflection in the mirror said otherwise,

"I asked how you're doing," she said.

I needed comfort food. Chocolate. A secret stash in my bedroom called to me. I grabbed a bag of M&Ms and made my way to the living room, where I flopped onto the sofa, juggling the candy and a water bottle. Noelle tended to be chatty. I might as well get comfortable. She's not my oldest sister, but definitely checks up on me the most. All three of my older sisters smother—I mean mother—me.

I took a deep breath, feeling much better now. "In other words, you want to know if I went to my appointment with Dr. Peterson today?"

Noelle laughed as if I had completely missed the mark. Silence. "Okay, yeah. Did you go?"

"I knew it! And, no. I didn't go—"

"Chrissy—"

"Because his receptionist rescheduled me for tomorrow. Wow, Elle. Give me some credit."

"Sorry. You've been doing so well. I don't want you to…" She paused, probably because she couldn't think of a graceful way of saying she didn't want me to take another nosedive into that dark abyss I'd lived in for the first two years after our parents died. A Christmastime car accident had claimed their lives, and I'd struggled through the holidays ever since. No way would I tell her about the little episode I'd just had. The attack had been minor, after all.

"I know, Elle. I don't want that, either. And I'm doing great." I took my voice up a notch to a happier pitch. "My marketing job's good; I live in the most beautiful green spot on earth—surrounded by mountains, hills and trees; I like my roommate, Kassandra—who wouldn't? She's hardly ever around, and when she is, she likes to clean; and I've got three awesome sisters." I paused. "Should I go on?"

"Are you dating anyone?" She knew I hated that question.

"Nope, but you'll be the first to know when I am." I knew she hated that answer.

"You don't have to get snarky about it. I'm interested, that's all."

"I know. But, Elle, we see each other almost every week. I think you'll know when there's someone I'm interested in. What about you? Are you dating anyone?"

Noelle had been through a brutal divorce. She deserved a great, non-cheating man to sweep her off her feet. Her ex was one of the reasons I'd sworn off men. Who needed that sort of pain?

## A word about the author...

Melinda S. Sanchez, grew up spellbound by the characters of wonderful books—Pippi Longstocking, Laura Ingalls Wilder, Kit Tyler, and many more.

She wrote her first book, in second grade, about two mice that got married. By age twelve she was prolific in writing poetry and stories and all through the years spent hours reading romance, biographies, and literature.

As an adult Melinda lived in the picturesque country of Italy and fell in love with the people, language, landscape, and history. She met her husband there, and together they have five beautiful grown children and five perfect grandchildren. They also have a house full of dogs, cats, exotic lizards and creatures, and birds—plenty of love and characters to inspire and keep Melinda spellbound and writing, writing, writing for a long time to come.

http://authormelindasanchez.com